DANCING TILL DAWN

Rebecca Paulinyi

This is a work of fiction. Names, characters, businesses, places, events and incidents are either the products of the author's imagination or used in a fictitious manner. Any resemblance to actual persons, living or dead, or actual events is purely coincidental.

Cover design by: German Creative

For Devon, the beautiful county I was born in, grew up in and married in.

CONTENTS

CHAPTER ONE

Mandy – 2022

The white wicker dressing table had belonged to Mandy since she had been a little girl. It had moved with her, whenever she was permanently settled. It had graced the bedroom she had shared with her husband, Laurie. After his passing, she had eventually moved to this cottage, because it was nearer to her son Caspian. And she had rebuilt her life.

Her fingers brushed over the green flowers embroidered on her white suit. The dressing table would not be moving after today, for her new husband would be joining her in this cottage. Perhaps his cuff links would join her rings in the floral bowl next to the mirror.

Another chapter of her life was beginning, and she felt excited about it. But that did not stop her thinking back, reminiscing on the chapters that had come before this one. Some good, some bad. Some which she thought would be longer. Some which she wished had been shorter. But they had all led her to today, when she was marrying Jonah Owens. She had put off marrying again for so many years, until it had finally felt right.

Until there had been a sign.

How strange it was to feel so happy and yet so nostalgically sorrowful at the same time. Her eyes blurred for a moment as she stared at herself in the mirror. The years had slipped by so quickly. Sometimes she still only felt eighteen, and yet she was fast approaching sixty and the lines on her face showed the laughter and the tears that she had lived through.

A knock on the door brought her back to reality, and she blinked rapidly and called for whoever it was to enter. She smiled at her niece, Isla, who was dressed in the sage green dress that Mandy had chosen for both her niece and her daughter-in-law to wear to this, her second wedding. She felt far too old for bridesmaids, but she wanted these two women who were so important to her to stand beside her as she took this next step.

Many, many years ago, it had been Isla's mother, Mandy's younger sister Anya, who had stood at the front of the church and watched Mandy marry Laurie.

But as the years slipped by, so the people around her changed. And she was so pleased that Isla had come to stay when her life had fallen to pieces, and that she had found so much happiness here in Devon.

There was something magical about the place, Mandy thought. She had never wanted to leave. And when she had left, she had yearned to return. She had been born here, and she was determined she would die here. But not, she hoped, for a long time to come.

"You look lovely," Isla said, a smile on her lips. "I just came to see if you needed anything."

Mandy shook her head. "No, I think I'm sorted. You look lovely too." Isla's relationship with the local bookshop owner seemed to be going from strength to strength, and Mandy hoped she would be attending their wedding one day in the future. She had been overjoyed when her darling son, Caspian, had found the wonderful

Beth to marry, and she felt similarly strong emotions about Isla's future happiness.

Isla furrowed her brow and took a seat on the wooden chair by the door. Often it had a jacket or scarf thrown across it, but today it was empty. Jonah would be moving in here after they had said their vows, and Mandy had made sure the cottage was spotless. Not that she thought Jonah would mind. He had stayed before, of course, but they had decided to wait to live together until after they were wed. A clear starting point to this next chapter.

"Are you okay?" Isla asked. She was certainly perceptive. She wasn't sure Caspian would have asked her that, or noticed the nostalgic mood she was in. But then, he did not really like discussing her marrying Jonah. He was supportive, yes, but that did not mean he was overly enthusiastic.

She could not blame him. He had hero-worshipped his father. And she too had put him on a pedestal for so many years. And it had been entirely deserved. Laurie was a wonderful man.

But he had been gone for a very long time.

"Oh yes," she said, smiling in reassurance. "Just... remembering."

Isla said nothing, and Mandy gazed off into the distance. "I was so excited, and terrified, when I married Laurie. And today..."

"If you don't want to go through with it, you don't have to," Isla said.

Tears had welled in Mandy's eyes without her realising, and she blinked them away and shook her head furiously. Isla was young. She had no reason, thankfully, to understand how torn Mandy felt. Excited for the future and yet wishing that the past had worked out differently.

"Oh no, it's not that," she said. "I'm excited today. And I love Jonah. But there are just so many memories... When you lose someone, even if you move on, you never really replace them."

She blinked away tears again, and glanced out of her bedroom window, towards the sea. She had always loved the sea. She had even named her son Caspian after the ocean.

Laurie had loved the sea too. Well, of course he had. It wouldn't have made much sense to be in the Navy if you hated the sea, after all.

Her sister had never felt the same affinity with the sea. She had been keen to leave this small town and spread her wings, to find love and a new life in a big city.

How Mandy missed her. Life brought so much joy, and yet so much loss. And today, when she was looking forward to so much, she also wanted to look back. To remember the good times, to remember the people that had shaped her life. Back to when everything had changed, in the summer of 1983.

Mandy – 1983

"Amanda, have you restocked the ice cream freezer? That last bus of tourists cleared us out."

"It's next on my list, Dad," Amanda called back. It was the hottest day so far that year, and she yearned for an ice cream herself. Her parents' little shop on Dartmouth harbour front was always busy in the summer, especially when the hot weather had tourists desperate for a lolly or a cold drink.

Once they closed up that evening, she thought she

might head down to the beach and treat herself to an evening swim to cool off after a hard day's work. She loved working in the shop, and meeting all the people who visited the area – but most of all she loved Devon, the county she called home. She could well understand why it was such a popular holiday destination. The beaches were, in her opinion, unrivalled – although, she supposed if she had been challenged, she would have had to admit to not having ventured very far to test this theory out.

She couldn't imagine living anywhere else. And so, even though her younger sister had tried to persuade her to apply to university, she had not done so. She was happy to stay here, to work in the shop, to take it over once Mum and Dad decided they didn't wish to run it any longer. One day she hoped to marry, to have children, to pass on her love of the sea and the sand to a little child who would call her Mummy.

It wasn't enough for Anya. She had applied to university, and was leaving for London in less than a month. It was hard to imagine life without her around, but it was harder to imagine leaving this place that she loved.

At five past five, Anya came bounding in, with a youthful exuberance that at eighteen was not calming down. While Anya had worked in the shop for many years, this summer she was enjoying her freedom, before starting her degree in English Literature.

"We're heading down to the beach as soon as Joanie's parents are home, so she doesn't have to babysit any more. Are you coming?"

Mandy grinned. "Definitely. Let me just grab my bikini. Are you driving?"

"As long as Mum lets me have the car!"

The little green Citroen was packed ten minutes later, with three of their friends crushed in the back. While it was common to learn to drive in Devon, it was not so common to have a car – and Mandy and Anya were lucky that their parents were generally happy for them to use theirs.

The August sun blazed down, making Mandy squint a little from her position in the front seat. She wished her sunglasses weren't buried at the bottom of the bag in the boot of the car.

They passed picturesque cottages as Bonni Tyler blared out of the radio. One day, Mandy fancied a little cottage like that, with a thatched roof and a view of the ocean. The perfect idyll in the beautiful county.

They had not discussed which beach they were going to, but Mandy was not surprised when Anya headed for Blackpool Sands. Out of the nearest beaches, it was the one Anya preferred, with its golden sands and crystal clear waters. Mandy was happy so long as she was on a beach, and the others didn't really get a say, since they had no way of getting anywhere without Mandy and Anya.

"Turn it up!" Georgina, who was squashed in the middle seat, shouted, and Mandy grinned and turned the dial so that Wham! could be heard for miles. She closed her eyes and let the sun warm her face, as the lyrics slipped from her mouth.

She loved the summer.

"I'll miss this," Danielle said behind her. "No nipping down to the beach once I'm in Bristol."

Mandy felt her smile falter. By the end of September, she would be the only one left. Anya, Danielle and Georgina were off to universities across the country. Joanie was doing a college course in childcare, but the commute meant she would be staying over in Exeter all week. Only Mandy had decided she was happy with what life here had to offer.

"You'll be down here swimming every night, Mandy," Georgina said. "We'll be jealous!"

"You'll all be here again by next summer, when it's hot," Mandy said. She glanced into the mirror and caught Georgina's eye. She did not think it was jealousy she saw there. It looked like pity. And that rankled.

There was no need for anyone to feel sorry for her. Mandy had chosen what she wanted to do once she left school, and this was it. Just as they had done. They were all younger than her, anyway – mainly from Anya's year, or the year in between.

"I'll miss you all," she said, as they turned into the little car park. "But I'm not sorry to be staying here."

The conversation disintegrated as they all piled out of the car. The beach was busy, despite the fact that it was almost dinner time, but they found a space to lay down their towels and strip off to their swimwear. The sun glistened on the water like glitter floating on the surface, and Mandy took a deep breath of the warm, salty air.

"It's certainly beautiful," Anya said, pulling her dark hair into a bun.

"I can't imagine anywhere more beautiful," Mandy said.

"Maybe not... But I'd like to get out there and see what there is, so I can judge properly."

Mandy smiled and squeezed her sister's hand. "Well, you'll have to let me know. Because I don't plan on leaving here. Now, I'll race you to the sea!"

CHAPTER TWO

Lee – 2022

"I'd forgotten," Lee Knight said through gritted teeth, "what this is like."

Her husband, James, gripped her hand tightly and did not complain when she squeezed it even tighter.

"It's been a few years," he said, his voice slightly strained. "But you were amazing when Holly was born, and you will be again. You can do anything, Lee."

As another contraction washed over her, Lee groaned and closed her eyes. She had been desperate to have another baby, but somehow had blocked out the memories of giving birth. Out in the corridor, her sister Beth was waiting, in case she was needed. Little Holly was with James' brother. Beth's mother-in-law Mandy had offered to have her, but James' sister had jumped in with the offer first. They were swamped with family, and extended family – and Lee loved it. She had spent her childhood with her sister and mother, with no one to turn to if things got tough. And then she had married a man who put his career above everything.

A man who did not care about family. And, in the end, had apparently not cared about her.

And now she was in the second half of her thirties, married to a man so wonderful she could hardly believe he was real. Their daughter was starting school, and their new little bundle of joy would be with them very soon.

Sooner than soon, she hoped, with the pain she was in.

"Let's just see how we're getting on, shall we?" the midwife said. Lee nodded and squeezed James's hand as another wave of pain washed over her.

The checks seemed to be taking longer than before and Lee forced herself to focus on a painting of a vase that hung on the wall. She didn't want to become alarmed when there was no need. And there would surely be no need. Everything had gone smoothly with Holly. And although she was a few years older, she wasn't that old.

The midwife called the doctor in, and Lee's eyes met James's. There was definitely worry there, and her heart began to race.

"Is everything okay?" she asked, gritting her teeth through another contraction.

"Things aren't progressing as quickly as we'd like," the midwife said, in a calm tone that did not stop Lee's anxiety from ramping up. "And baby's heart rate has dropped a little."

"What does that-" Lee began, gripping James's hand more tightly, not through pain this time but through fear.

"I am going to advise an emergency c-section, Mrs Knight," the doctor said, meeting Lee's eyes. Lee swallowed. That was not part of the plan. She liked to have a plan, and this was something she had not wanted.

"Is that necessary?" she asked, her voice weak.

"We could wait a little longer, but not much. I would be much happier to have baby out now. I know this is not what you wanted, but I think-"

"Is it the safest option?" James interrupted.

The doctor's eyes moved from Lee to James and she nodded. "Yes, Mr Knight. In my professional opinion, a caesarean section now would be the safest option for Mrs Knight and the baby."

Lee swallowed, and turned to her husband. His blue eyes were wide.

"It's your choice, Lee."

"But you think I should have it?"

"If it's safest for you, and the baby, then yes."

Lee nodded. He was right, of course. If the professional thought it was the best option, it was what she would do, even though she hated the thought of it.

"Okay." She turned to the doctor. "Okay."

The doctor immediately began writing something on her clipboard. "Excellent. The anesthesiologist will be in to explain everything, and we'll get you prepped. Please, try not to worry Mrs Knight. You'll be holding your little one soon."

Tears began to roll down Lee's face as she and James were left briefly alone. "This isn't how I wanted to have this baby," she said.

"I know," James said, his voice shaking a little. "I do. But we just have to do what's best for you and what's best for this baby. They do c-sections all the time. It will be fine. And I will look after you afterwards, you won't have to lift a finger."

Lee laughed through her tears. Considering how overprotective he had been in both pregnancies, she could well imagine that she wouldn't be allowed to lift a finger.

"You are the strongest person I know, Lee. You can do this. I promise you. I love you."

***

James knew he needed to be strong for Lee, no matter how terrified he was himself. She was always so calm and measured, and when she looked panicked, he knew he needed to step up.

He held her hand while they put in the spinal block, avoiding looking in case the needle made him feel squeamish. He always felt a bit off in hospitals, even though, in his work as a police officer, he was not unused to being in them.

It was definitely worse, though, when it was someone you loved. The anesthesiologist had talked them through what would happen, but James didn't think he'd taken much in. He was quite surprised at the number of people in the room, and at how calm they all seemed.

He was worried he might be sick himself. Lee was chatting to one of the nurses, who seemed to be trying to distract her with questions about Holly and Lee's work. James was grateful. He needed to get his head straight so that he could be there for Lee, and for their new baby.

"It feels so strange," Lee whispered, and he realised she was speaking to him and forced his mind to focus on the here and now.

"What does, love?"

"Not being able to feel my legs."

"I bet."

"Can you see?" she asked, jerking her head towards the screen that stopped her being able to view her lower half.

"I could, if I tried," James said. "But I have no plans to look."

Lee laughed. "Don't faint on me, will you."

He didn't have it in him to laugh, but he smiled,

although he didn't think it was that ridiculous a notion.

But he needed to be here for her, so he would not look, and he would not faint.

Things moved quickly then. Times were called out and written on the board, and several people were gathered around Lee's lower half.

James focused on his wife's face. He stroked her hair, and tried to smile. "Can you believe we'll have two children very soon?"

Lee shook her head, tears welling up in her eyes. She was not one to cry easily, and he wondered if it was the tiredness or the hormones or just overwhelm at the situation they were in.

"We didn't exactly follow the plan," James said with a half-laugh. "If you'd written down your ten-year plan, I doubt I'd have been on it."

"Oh, you definitely would have been," Lee said.

"Well, not the way things happened between us then, hey? Meeting when we did, so soon after your marriage had broken down. And getting pregnant so quickly..."

Lee gave a watery smile. "No. Probably not. But it's all worked out for the best, hasn't it?"

James smiled properly then, and took her hand and kissed it. "The very, very best Lee. And this may not be the way we planned, but it's going to be perfect, you'll see."

It was like they had forgotten just where they were, but then there was a wail, and they both turned their heads to look at the blue screen. Lee couldn't have looked over if she'd wanted to, but James made a very concerted effort not to. He wanted to see his baby, but he wasn't so keen to see where they'd pulled him out of.

"A healthy little boy," the doctor said, and James

could tell from his eyes that he was smiling, in spite of the face mask covering his mouth. "Congratulations Mrs Knight, Mr Knight."

They held him up, a chunky, red baby boy with no hair and strong-sounding lungs. "We'll just clean him up, and get you sewn up," the nurse said. "Would Dad like to come and trim the cord?"

James looked to Lee.

"Up to you," she said, her face pale but her eyes shining with joy.

"Okay," he said, following the nurse, who showed him what to do. He couldn't take his eyes off his son. He looked bigger than Holly had done, more robust. How strange that he was the one who'd had everyone worried. But now he was here, kicking his little legs, waiting to meet his mother on the outside.

◆ ◆ ◆

It was hard to lie there, unable to move, knowing her son was metres away, while they stitched her up. Of course, she didn't have a choice, but she was anxious for them to bring him back over.

When they finally did, and placed him in her arms, she felt complete. That rush of love that she had felt with Holly hit her once more with this little one, and it was like her heart grew to accommodate all that extra love.

"Hello little one," she whispered. "Mummy loves you very much."

She looked up at James and her heart felt like it might burst at the love in his eyes.

"Well done, my darling," he said, pressing a kiss to her forehead, and then one on the forehead of their little boy. "You did it."

"We did it," she said. "I cannot wait for you to meet your big sister," she told the tiny baby, who was beginning to root around in hunger. "She is going to love you so much."

"You've got a very big family, little man," James whispered. "And they are all going to be thrilled to meet you."

CHAPTER THREE

Mandy – 1983

"Remember Tommy, that I went for dinner with last week?" Anya said, as she and Mandy sat together in the garden, enjoying the end of the summer sunshine. The deck chairs were left out all through the summer months, although Mandy was sure she and Anya were the only ones who used them. She had a day off from the shop, and she was keen to spend it with her sister, before she left for London.

"Oh yes," Mandy said, sipping from her lukewarm can of coke. "The one on holiday with his parents?"

Anya laughed and shook her head. Mandy didn't feel it was her fault she couldn't keep up. Anya had never had a serious relationship, but she'd had a stream of men wanting to date her for years.

"No, the one at the naval college."

Mandy nodded. She could picture him now, a tall fellow with blond hair. He hadn't been wearing his uniform, otherwise she definitely would have remembered where he had come from. Britannia Royal Naval College brought much excitement and many eligible young men into the area. In fact, it was rather surprising that this was the first naval man that Anya had been on a date with. Well, as far as Mandy knew, anyway.

Most recently, two of the royal princes – one the future king, Charles – had attended the college. At school she and her friends had joked about running into them, and becoming princesses – but of course, they'd never even caught sight of them.

"Well, he's invited me to the naval ball."

Mandy surveyed her sister over her sunglasses. An invitation to the naval ball was a big deal. The cadets wore their uniforms, the ladies wore fine ball gowns, and they paraded through the town beforehand, garnering the attention of locals and tourists alike. Mandy had seen people on their way to the ball many times, and she was a little jealous of her sister's chance to go.

"That's exciting," she said, not letting the twinge of jealousy leak into her voice. "Do you have enough money for a new dress?"

Anya nodded. "All those hours working in the shop weren't for nothing! Do you have enough?"

Mandy frowned. "If you need me to lend you the money, then I can-"

Anya laughed. She was always laughing. Nothing ever seemed to get her down for long. "No, silly. Tommy has a friend who's looking for a date, and I thought you might be keen to go too."

Mandy grinned. She didn't tend to date much; she was nowhere near as outgoing as her younger sister. Making conversation with a young man she did not know made her a little nervous. But experiencing the naval ball, and with Anya, was worth it.

"Definitely," she said, joy bubbling up inside her.

"I don't know much about his friend, I'm afraid," she said. "But I think every man in a uniform is handsome, so I'm sure you'll have a good night."

Mandy rolled her eyes. "I know you do. Maybe it would do you good to be a bit more discerning!"

Anya tapped her sister's leg. "I'll settle down one day. For now, I'm very happy to just have fun. Besides, I leave for London soon. No point dating anyone seriously."

◆ ◆ ◆

Mandy's savings were fairly substantial, with so much time spent working, and little interest in spending it. When she had first seen the ocean-blue, a-line dress, she had wanted to wear it. But then she had seen the price, and she had baulked. She had never spent so much on an item of clothing before. Anya had made her try it on, and when she saw herself in the soft chiffon, it was hard to walk away from it.

"That's the dress, Mandy. You look incredible."

Mandy smiled at her sister's compliment. "This guy is only going on a date with me because he's friends with your date. So I'm not sure it matters what I look like."

"Nonsense," Anya said, twirling in a hot pink gown that set off her summer tan. "Dress to impress. No matter why you're there. You never know who you might meet!"

On the evening of the ball, Mandy rather wished she liked the taste of alcohol. Perhaps a stiff drink would have calmed the nerves in her stomach. But she had never enjoyed it, and a big night like tonight did not seem like a good time to take it up.

Tommy, Anya's date, met them outside, dressed in his dark naval uniform with its peaked cap. His buttons gleamed and his shoes shone, and Mandy would later admit to her sister that he did look rather handsome.

He kissed Anya on the cheek, and after a pause did the same to Mandy. She could smell his cologne. Had he forgotten that she was supposed to be accompanying his friend? What would happen if the friend already had a date? Would she have to go home, in this dress that she had spent so much money on, and wait to hear of the excitement of the night from Anya?

"Lovely to meet you," he said.

"And you," Mandy said. She had seen him from a distance, picking Anya up, but never actually spoken to him.

She was just about to ask him if his friend had other plans, when a tall, dark-haired cadet appeared behind Tommy.

And Mandy could have sworn her heart stopped beating.

His dark hair peaked out from under his cap, and his eyelashes fluttered as he looked from Tommy to Anya to Mandy.

Their eyes met and Mandy's mouth went dry. He was the most beautiful man she had ever seen. There was no way her mind could form words, and so she was inordinately grateful when Tommy made the introductions.

"Laurie, thought you'd got lost!" he said, clapping his friend on the back.

"Jim's hat got taken again," he said. "I was helping him find it."

"Poor bloke," Tommy said. "Anyway, this is Anya, who I was telling you about, and her sister, Amanda."

Mandy smiled and when he offered his hand to shake, she took it, even though she felt like her skin might burst into flames at the contact. Never before had she been rendered speechless by a man. Perhaps the uniform had a stronger power than she had realised.

"You look beautiful, ladies," Laurie said. But in her heart, the words were only for her. She had never felt this possessive over a compliment, over a man, but for once she wanted to be noticed above her sister.

"It's traditional to go for a drink in town, before the ball, apparently," Tommy said. "Shall we?" He offered his arm to Anya, who took it gladly, giving Mandy a wide-eyed grin before walking ahead of them.

Laurie offered his arm to Mandy, and she wound hers through it, hoping she wasn't going to make a fool of herself.

"You live in Dartmouth then, Amanda?" he asked.

"Only my parents call me Amanda," she said softly.

"Oh, sorry," he said. "What should I call you?"

"Everyone else calls me Mandy."

"Mandy it is then."

"I've lived here all my life," she said, wondering if that would seem sad to a man like him, who was surely well-travelled.

"It's such a beautiful place," he said. "I don't blame you."

She glanced up at him, and then caught her foot on a paving stone and quickly looked away. Apparently she could not be trusted to walk and look at him.

Thankfully, he did not comment on her clumsiness.

"It is. I couldn't imagine being away from the sea."

She could hear the smile in his voice, even though she didn't dare look up at him again. "I never want to be away from the sea, either. Although I suppose I mainly want to be on it."

"Well, in your chosen profession, that's probably a good thing!"

They walked along the waterfront, the town filled with women in ball gowns accompanied by cadets in their naval uniforms, and passersby watching them. People hung out of windows to get a look, and for once Mandy did not feel shy. Wearing this dress, and being on the arm of this handsome man, was a heady feeling indeed. Excitement was in the air, and when they reached a pub and took seats outside, Anya reached across and squeezed her hand.

Mandy could not help but grin back. Magic filled the air, and she felt part of something incredible. Tonight was a night she did not think she would ever forget, no matter how long she lived or where her life took her.

CHAPTER FOUR

Beth and Caspian – 2022

"Thanks so much for the lift, Mandy," Beth said, embracing her mother-in-law. So often people complained about their mothers-in-law, but Beth felt that she had lucked out. Mandy was a dream. And so much easier than Beth's own mother, whose impossibly high standards made it hard for them to have the uncomplicated relationship she did with Mandy.

"You two enjoy yourselves," Mandy said, standing on tiptoes to hug her son.

Caspian kissed his mother on the head and hugged her tightly for a moment before releasing her. "Look after yourself, Mum. And Jonah."

Beth smiled. It had been almost seven months since his mother had married Jonah, his former piano teacher, a widower that Mandy had known for many years. Beth knew her husband had struggled with his mother remarrying after it being just the two of them for so long. And at the thought of his father being replaced, even though, when Beth pushed the point, he didn't want his mother to be in mourning forever.

But now, if they went away, he didn't need to worry about her. When they had moved to Scotland for a brief time, he had worried about Mandy being left alone. Now they wanted to travel, as research for Beth's latest novel, and both were happy that Mandy was no longer alone. She also had her niece, Caspian's cousin Isla for company – although she increasingly spent her time with her boyfriend, Luca.

"Let me know you land, won't you," Mandy said.

Caspian rolled his eyes but grinned anyway. "Is there any age I will reach that you won't be making me let you know when I get somewhere?"

Mandy reached up to touch a hand to his cheek. "No. You will always be my baby, I'm afraid, no matter how old you get."

"How did you cope before mobile phones?"

"Pay phones," Mandy said. "And I suppose a lot of worried parents! Now, come on, you don't want to be late. I know it's a tiny airport, but you still need to get through security."

With Caspian wheeling the bags, Beth double-checked their passports and boarding cards. Her stomach churned with excitement. Her books were selling well enough that she could justify this trip to the Greek islands as research, as well as a well-deserved holiday for her and Caspian. Since they could both work remotely, the trip had no end date, and the freedom to be able to disappear off for an indeterminate amount of time thrilled her. She would miss Mandy, and of course her sister Lee and her children, four-year-old Holly and tiny baby Harry. But the wonder of modern technology would ensure they kept in touch, and they would all be waiting upon their return.

At the gate, Caspian pulled her into a kiss that sent her spine tingling. Even now, after four years, he could make her feel like fireworks were exploding in her chest, with just a simple kiss.

Slightly breathless, she looked up into his eyes, losing herself in his smouldering gaze.

"What was that for?" she asked.

"Just because," he said with a shrug.

As they boarded their flight, Beth felt like the luckiest woman alive. For so many years, she had felt like her life was going nowhere. She had worked simply to live, and had never really enjoyed any of the temporary jobs she had done. She had always been the failure of the family, compared to her powerhouse of a sister who had been made a partner in her law firm before she was thirty, and was married to a doctor. She had not been able to find a man who made her feel anything at all.

And now... Her life was entirely changed. So was her sister's, for that matter. It turned out that no matter how perfect things looked on the outside, someone could want a different life. Beth loved writing, and the fact that she was making money at it was thrilling. She loved living in Devon, and swimming with Caspian in the ocean every summer evening. She loved being close to her sister and her niece and nephew, having this network of family that she had never had before. They'd even reconnected with their father, who they'd always thought had run off and abandoned them, and now had a relationship with him.

She had everything she could have wished for.

As they soared across the sky, the clouds like white candy floss beneath the wings of the plane, Beth snuggled into Caspian's side. He was reading a novel, a rare occurrence for the workaholic, but she was happy just people-watching. In the opposite aisle, a woman bounced a baby on her lap, showing him the view from the window. Beth smiled, thinking of little Harry, and of chatty Holly. She loved her nephew and niece, although she wished people would stop asking her when she and Caspian were having children. They were perfectly happy as they were – and yet apparently that was an unacceptable answer. She wondered what would happen if she gave them an answer they didn't want to hear. Told them that she and Caspian had been trying to conceive moments before they'd walked in, or that they could not get pregnant. Neither were true, but saying that they were perfectly content being child-free didn't seem to be understood by most people. If they had a child, they would not have the freedom to disappear to Greece for a few weeks to research a novel, would they? They had both acknowledged that, in the future, they would possibly want to have children. But Beth was only thirty-three. They had time. She wasn't going to rush into something she didn't want just in case. Lee had wanted to be a mother since Beth could remember, and although Beth thought her sister missed work, she loved raising her children.

Everyone had a path in life that was right for them, and for Beth and Caspian, this was the right path for now.

"Good book?" she asked when Caspian glanced down at her.

"Pretty decent," he said. "Have you got a plan for this Grecian book you're writing next, or are you just seeing what happens when inspiration strikes?"

Beth's first novel had been written entirely off the cuff, with no plan at all. But now she tried to have a rough idea of who the killer was in the murder mysteries she so enjoyed writing.

"The murderer is going to have a yacht I think," she

said. "So we'll need to go out on one I guess."

"Without a murderer on it, I hope," Caspian said with a wry grin.

"That's probably for the best," Beth said with a giggle, stretching her legs and glancing at her watch. "You can swim in the sea twice a day if you like, if the weather is as nice as it's supposed to be!"

"With our hotel being practically on the beach, I'm hoping to spend more time in the water than out of it!"

CHAPTER FIVE

Mandy – 1983

Mandy was surprised at how easily the conversation flowed between them, considering how tongue-tied she had felt upon first seeing him. Whilst she was often shy, she didn't usually find herself blushing and tripping over words – and yet that was exactly what happened every time she met Laurie's dark eyes across the table.

The sun was low in the sky, but the streets were still busy. Every now and then she heard a passerby commenting on all the pretty dresses, or how handsome the cadets looked in their uniforms. She did not normally like being the centre of attention, but tonight it made her feel a little bit special. And the attention Laurie was paying her only increased that.

"How long have you been in Dartmouth for?" Mandy asked, her finger catching a bead of condensation as it ran down the side of her glass of lemonade.

"Just over three months," Laurie said. "But I'll be honest, we're so busy over at Britannia that I haven't seen much of it."

Mandy was tempted to offer to show him round, but bit back the words. He was surely too busy. And besides, a handsome man like him surely had a girl in every port. He would think she was ridiculous for suggesting they spend more time together. She was just here because Tommy wanted to take her sister – she shouldn't think anything more of it.

"That's a shame," she said eventually. "And what's next?"

"We'll be back and forth for the next few months," he said. "Out on the ship for a bit and then back for training. But eventually I'm aiming to be a Cadet Deck Officer. Travel the world."

Mandy smiled. "How exciting." She could see in his eyes how thrilled he was at the prospect. How small he must think her dreams were. She didn't want to leave this place that she called home. "Your parents must be so proud."

"I like to think they would be," he said, raising his bottle of beer to his lips. "I was raised by my grandparents."

"Oh, I'm sorry," she said, blushing at her misstep.

"You didn't know," he said. "My grandparents love telling everyone their grandson is in the Navy." When he smiled his eyes lit up and Mandy felt a sparkle in her heart. Never before had she felt such an instant connection and she was intent on enjoying it. Would she feel this way again, in the future? She hoped so, but perhaps it was just a magical night of being young and free with a handsome young man and a life full of promise.

When she glanced over at her sister, Anya also seemed to be basking in the joy of being young. Her cheeks were red and her eyes were bright, and when she met her sister's eye she beamed.

"You're lucky to have such a close family," Laurie said. "I always wished I had a brother."

"Some of my friends hate their siblings," she said, very aware of Anya listening in. "But I think I got pretty lucky!"

"You'll miss me when I leave next month."

And then the conversation grew to encompass the four of them, and Mandy felt a twinge of sadness. She would definitely miss her sister once she left. Would her love of Devon be enough without her sister and her friends for company?

"We should head off," Laurie said, glancing at a large watch on his wrist. He glanced around. "Everyone else is starting to make a move."

Laurie offered his arm, and a thrill shot through Mandy's body as she entwined hers with his. No matter where her life took her, she did not think she would ever forget the feeling of walking through her beloved Dartmouth in a beautiful dress on the arm of this very handsome Navy cadet.

CHAPTER SIX

Isla and Luca – 2022

Isla stretched her legs out in Luca's king-sized bed and gave herself a moment to fully wake from the dream she had been having. It was not a particularly pleasant one. She was sat in the office that she had worked in for many years, watching her then-boyfriend tapping away at his computer in his glass office. Fully visible, but unobtainable.

She shivered, even though the day was warm. How had she not realised that he did not love her? That she had nothing, and that when he ended things, she would be homeless, penniless, all alone.

But it was just a dream. She had lived that nightmare, and she had come out the other side. Her broken heart had been healed thanks to the kindness of her family, and the love of the man she now happily called her boyfriend.

Technically, she still lived with her aunt Mandy, in the next village of Strete. But in reality she spent most of her nights with Luca in his flat that overlooked the water. In the eight months since Mandy had married Jonah, Isla had repeatedly insisted she would find her own place. But Aunt Mandy had been just as insistent that there was no need to waste money on rent. And it was hard for Isla not to agree. She had managed to build up a little nest egg thanks to working at Luca's bookshop, Lee's Totnes café, and editing Beth's novels. But when she had come here, she'd had nothing at all. And she liked the security of a little money in her account, of not being in her overdraft.

Besides, she spent so much time at Luca's, the rent really would have felt wasted. And yet she could not bring herself to move in with him, even when he asked, even though she loved him. For one, this had been his house with his wife, who had sadly passed away. Moving in here did not seem right. And for another, never again did she want to have her life resting on the knife-edge of a man's whims. What if he decided he did not want to be with her anymore? Would she once again be homeless, and jobless? No. She wanted to be with him, but she also wanted to maintain enough of her independence so that if things went wrong, she could deal with her heartbreak without worrying where she was going to sleep at night.

She was quite happy working three jobs, even if it left her rather exhausted. Luca wasn't so keen on it, and she had taken this day off to make him happy, because he had suggested it. In fact, right at this moment he was in the bookshop, training up a new member of staff so that they could have days off together. She smiled at the thought, and padded out to the kitchen to make a cup of tea and watch the boats bobbing on the water. Dartmouth was so beautiful. She had worried she would find it too quiet after living in cities her whole life, but she felt truly at home here. And knowing that her mother had grown up in the area just made her feel even closer to her. How she missed her.

It was nice to be able to talk about her with Aunt Mandy. She was the only person who really remembered her. Who knew her even better than Isla had done. Her cousin Caspian didn't remember his aunt that well, just as Isla didn't remember his father, her uncle Laurie, particularly clearly. How cruel life seemed to be, with them both losing a parent so young. With Isla's father having disappeared from their lives when she was just a baby, the death of her mother had left her entirely alone.

How grateful she was now to have Aunt Mandy, and Caspian, and the whole extended family around her.

With a steaming mug of tea in her hand, Isla settled in her favourite armchair and pulled out the latest manuscript that Beth had sent her to edit. She had promised she would take a day off, and she did plan to head to the shop, and see Luca, and hopefully go out for lunch with him. But she loved her editing work, and she was happy to lose herself in it for an hour or two while she was alone. She was excited for the new series Beth was starting, set in the Greek islands. She would miss her cousin and his wife while they were travelling, but she was thrilled by Beth's success. Both for Beth's sake, and, a little selfishly, for Isla's own. The better Beth did with her writing, the more she wanted Isla to edit – and Isla was quite keen to build up the editing work so that it eventually was her sole profession.

Her heart felt light as she dived into the world Beth had weaved, filled with intrigue, and history, and mystery.

CHAPTER SEVEN

Lee and James – 2022

"Are you okay to pick Holly up from school, if I drop her off?" James asked at six that morning. Holly was still asleep, but baby Harry was feeding contentedly, while Lee sipped the coffee that James had brought up for her.

"Yeah, that's fine. I was hoping to stop by the café today, just check everything is ticking over."

"You know Gina always has everything under control," James said as he dressed in his police uniform. "You don't need to worry."

Lee tried to bite back irritation. James was wonderful. She knew he was only looking out for her, wanting to make sure she didn't overdo it with a four-month-old baby in tow. But she missed her work. She missed the café, she missed the little law firm she had set up, she missed seeing people and talking about topics other than baby spit-up and nappies and how many hours of sleep she'd had the night before.

Guilt washed over her. She loved her children. She had been desperate to be a mother, and these two wonderful humans she had birthed were a dream come true.

But she could not help feeling a little jealous of James going off to work and still being a person, as well as an amazing dad.

"I know," she said. "I just like to pop in."

He leant across and kissed her lips, careful not to disturb Harry's feed. "I'll miss you today," he said. "It'll be a late one I'm afraid."

"I'll try to cook dinner without burning the house down," she joked. When he was home, James did all the cooking, because he was so much better in the kitchen. Before him, Lee had been adept at ordering takeaways. But her life was so much different than it was then. Back then, her career had been more important than anything – and she had only realised that her marriage was falling apart when it was too late.

She would never make that mistake again.

She pushed away the seed of irritation and put it down to a lack of sleep. Soon Holly would be up, and she wanted to be up and ready to enjoy breakfast with her daughter before she lost her to school for the day.

◆ ◆ ◆

"You've got swimming at school today, Holls," James reminded his daughter. He glanced in the rear-view mirror and smiled at the sight of her in her uniform, watching the cars passing them by. She was an inquisitive little girl, and always happy. He never tired of spending time with her. When she had started school earlier that year, he had felt sad that her hours would belong to them for the rest of her childhood. When he went to work, he wished he could stay with his children a little longer.

He had always enjoyed his job as a police officer. It was what he had always wanted to do. But lately... Lately there seemed to be more and more stress, increasing paperwork, and so many reasons he couldn't get home to his family on time. He hated missing bedtime, especially on the days he knew he would be gone before Holly woke up the next morning.

He sighed, and Holly's head whipped around.

"Are you sad, Daddy?" she asked, with the slight lisp she always seemed to have when saying an 's' sound.

He shook his head. "No, sweetheart. I'm never sad when I'm with you!"

She seemed happy with that answer, but once he had dropped her off at school, he revisited it again.

Was he sad?

No. He loved Lee, he loved his children, and his life was a happy one. They were financially comfortable, and were surrounded by family. His dad had been struggling with cancer for a while, and that concerned him, but he was always one to look for the positives.

He was not sad. He just wanted to spend more time with his children. But they needed one of them to be out earning a decent wage, and while Lee was on maternity leave, that was him. Perhaps when she was thinking of going back to work, he would suggest a sabbatical. Instead of sending Harry to nursery, or asking his mum or Beth to watch him. Yes, in a few months he would raise that, and he would be able to tuck his children in at night and wake them in the morning.

But for now, he knew a mountain of paperwork awaited him.

CHAPTER EIGHT

Mandy – 1983

The domed ceiling had intricate designs on it, and Mandy almost tripped trying to look up at them. Thankfully Laurie had her arm, and he tightened his grip as she stumbled and then smiled down at her. Her cheeks flushed, both in embarrassment and because of the close contact between them.

"This place is spectacular," she said, a little breathless. "I've never been inside before."

Laurie glanced around. "I suppose it is. You stop noticing after a few days!"

They were offered a tray with glasses of champagne, and instead of refusing, Mandy took one. She sipped the golden liquid, and although the taste made her wince a little, the bubbles tingled in her mouth, and she went back for another sip.

She wore low heels, and they tapped on the wooden floors as they made their way over to a window, to wait for the music to start. The band in the corner seemed to be getting ready, and the room was steadily filling with gowns of all colours and rows of smart dark uniforms with crisp white shirts peeking out.

"What's your plan, once your sister has left for university?" Laurie asked, sipping his own champagne.

The words stuck in her mouth. Here, in this setting, her dreams suddenly felt unimportant.

"I'll stay here," she said softly. "When my parents retire, I'll take over their shop I suppose."

"Do you like working in the shop?" he asked.

"I like the people," she said. "You meet all sorts. And I like knowing my parents aren't struggling alone."

"But you're not wedded to being in a shop forever?"

"I like to sew," she said, confiding something in him that she hadn't even mentioned to Anya. "I suppose, if I had a choice, I would stay in Devon, still see people, but sew for a living."

"That doesn't sound so impossible," he said, his kind eyes locked on hers.

"It sounds like a pretty small dream," she said, glancing down at the floor.

He hooked his finger under her chin and lifted her head, and her skin felt like it might burst into flames.

"Don't put yourself down," he said. "You know what you want, and you're going after it. There's plenty of people just meandering through life with no clue what will make them happy."

A grin spread across Mandy's face. His lips were inches from hers and she felt an overwhelming urge to press hers to his. Not that she would ever be that brave. But when his eyes locked on hers and he spoke in that deep, chocolatey voice, she felt as though he could see right into her soul.

Suddenly the band started to play in earnest, jolting them out of their moment. When she glanced at Anya, her sister simply smirked and raised her eyebrows.

Mandy felt her cheeks flush, but looked back to Laurie all the same. He had let go of her chin, and he was still smiling. He offered her his hand. "Would you like to dance?"

Mandy nodded. She couldn't trust herself to speak. He led her out onto the dance floor, and he put her arms around his neck, and they swayed to the slow opening bars of 'Endless Love'. She didn't really know how to dance, but it didn't matter. She didn't even know if she was moving in time with the music. All she could think about was his hands on her waist, the smile on his lips, and how she would remember this night forever.

CHAPTER NINE

Beth and Caspian – 2022

Caspian reclined on the sun lounger and glanced over at his wife. She was far paler than he was, and was covered in sun cream as well as a cover-up, to avoid burning. In her hands, as there so often was, was a notebook. He wondered how many authors these days spent hours writing things by hand. She had a laptop, of course, and her final draft was typed – but for every new book she bought a new notebook and wrote much of it by hand.

The waves lazily caressed the beach before pulling out again, and Caspian looked out to the horizon. He had always loved the sea. It was part of why he had continued to have Devon as his base, even when he had been travelling across the country for work. That, and he had not wanted to leave his mum alone.

But she was okay now. She was happy and settled and she had someone else to look out for her. And however awkward he felt about her remarrying, he knew that was the most important thing.

It was hard sometimes to remember his father. He had died when Caspian was only seven, nearly thirty years earlier. He knew he looked like him. He remembered wearing his father's naval cap, and wanting to join the Navy like him when he was older.

Once he was older, he'd realised it wasn't the life for him. As much as he loved the sea, and his father, he liked being his own boss. He enjoyed the publicity business, and his company had quickly become successful. He had the freedom to work the hours he wanted, travel where he wanted, to support his wife in her dream of being an author. They could disappear for a month on a research trip and he could enjoy the warm seas and work whenever time allowed.

He hoped his dad would be proud of him, even though he had not followed his footsteps into the Navy. He was happily living the life that suited him, and he was madly in love with the woman who lay on a sun lounger beside him.

"Will you come in for a swim in a minute?" he asked.

She looked up from her notebook and flashed him a wide grin. Her blonde hair glinted in the sunlight. "Let me just finish this scene, then I'd love to. Can you top up my sun cream first?"

She pulled off the floral cover-up to reveal a black bikini that flattered her petite body. While Caspian poured sun cream into his hands, she leant forwards and away from him, continuing to furiously scribble as he massaged the lotion into her back. He couldn't resist pressing a kiss to her neck and she giggled.

"You're very distracting, you know," she said.

"That's why I'm here," he said with a laugh. "You'd be bored without me."

She put down the notebook and turned to press her lips against his. "I wouldn't want to be anywhere without you, Caspian. You know that."

For many years, Caspian had shortened his name,

feeling self-conscious over how unusual it was. But Beth had always said she loved it, and when it fell from her lips, he loved it too.

They walked down to the sea hand-in-hand, the sun warming their backs. They had met under a moonlit sky, in a sea far colder than this one. And ever since that moment, he had been unable to get Beth off his mind.

How lucky he felt to have met her out swimming that evening, and to have run into her again when she was working, and to have ended up dating her. They so easily could have passed one another by, never crossed paths, and then where would his life be now?

It wasn't worth thinking about.

Life was such a gamble, and he felt like he had won the jackpot.

◆ ◆ ◆

They had been away for three weeks when Beth showed signs of being ill. Before that, everything had been going great. Every day they had enjoyed the sunshine, swam in the sea together, visited someplace new. After a week in one hotel, they moved on to another, loving the fact that they were free to go wherever they wished, to be as long as they liked. They visited a rural area of the island of Rhodes, because Beth was keen to set a scene of the book in a rural farmhouse.

The first day that she was sick, they assumed it was food poisoning. Caspian sympathised, and brought her peppermint tea and crackers, and didn't leave her side. The next day, when she felt no better, she insisted he go for a swim in the sea, and not spend all day in the air-conditioned hotel room with her.

When she had felt sick and achy and exhausted for

almost a week, they both began to feel a little concerned.

"I think you should see a doctor," Caspian said, not for the first time that week.

Beth sighed. "I told you, I don't want to spend all day sat in some hospital, waiting to be seen. I'm sure I'll feel better tomorrow."

"You say that every day Beth, and I'm getting worried."

Beth's stomach rolled again. "Okay. If I'm not better tomorrow, I promise we can see a doctor."

Caspian smiled, but Beth could see it did not quite reach his eyes. In truth, she was a little worried too. She couldn't remember being ill for this long since she was a child.

"Before we do, Beth... Is there any chance..."

Beth frowned. "Any chance of what?" she asked.

"Well, I know we're careful. But with you being sick so much... Is there any chance you could be pregnant?"

Panic washed over her. They were careful. She did not want children yet. It hadn't even crossed her mind that feeling like this could possibly be a sign...

"I don't think so," she said slowly. "I don't think the dates add up. And surely you don't feel this ill because you're pregnant?"

Caspian shrugged. "I don't know. Got no experience with it, as you know. I just thought, before we see a doctor..."

Beth nodded and swallowed. "Yeah. Can you... Do you think you can get me a pregnancy test?"

Caspian nodded. "Most shops have some English. And if not I'll just show them a photo. Is there any specific type or..."

Beth's heart pounded in panic at the conversation.

"I don't know, do I! I've not got some in-built intuition about these things."

"Sorry…" Caspian murmured. "I'll go now."

Beth reached out and grabbed his hand. "No, I'm sorry. I'm just…"

"I know," Caspian said, pressing a kiss to her clammy forehead. "It'll all be okay, I promise. No matter what."

CHAPTER TEN

Mandy – 1983

They danced until Mandy could no longer feel her feet and then they took another glass of champagne out into the yard, and stood beneath the inky black sky, talking and drinking and laughing.

He would be going out to sea soon, he had made that clear. Even if he was interested in her, there was no way they could start dating. And she thought it unlikely he would be interested. For an evening of dancing and conversation, perhaps she was enough, but not for anything more long-term.

She had always thought that one day she would date, and settle down, and marry, and have children. But she had not really put any thought into when, or who this husband would be, or where she would meet him. She had quite happily been pottering on with her life, assuming that everything would work out as it was supposed to.

And then suddenly, this beautiful man had turned her head, and made her wonder if there were other such men out there in the world. Laurie would be gone soon, off on a ship, and then out at sea more permanently, with surely no mind to settling down. He could have his pick of the girls, and girls all over the world too. What could boring Amanda Moss offer him, truly?

"I'm so glad you came," Laurie said, as they sipped champagne and looked out over the water. The bubbles, and the rare intake of alcohol, were going to her head. Her eyes lingered on his lips for far too long, and then jumped back to his beautiful, dark eyes. "I'm so glad you invited me," she said, the alcohol making her a little more honest than perhaps she might have been. "I had a magical evening."

Laurie beamed. "It's not over yet," he said, clinking his glass with hers. "You're not going to bail out early on me, are you?" he said, a twinkle in his eye

Mandy shook her head. "I'm not ready to leave yet," she said.

"I know you said you live with your parents. You don't have a curfew, or anything, do you? I'm not going to get you in trouble?"

Mandy laughed and blushed, a little embarrassed at how young he obviously thought she was. "I'm nearly twenty-one," she said, holding his gaze. "I can stay out as late as I like."

She swore Laurie's glance darted to her lips, before coming back to hold her gaze once more.

"Whereas I am the grand old age of twenty-five," he said. "And I generally cannot stay out as late as I like. The Navy has pretty strict rules."

"I can imagine," Mandy said. She did not think it would be a good life for her. There was a women's division of the Navy, she knew that. But even if she had wanted to leave Devon, she did not think a life of rules and regulations was what she envisaged for herself.

"But tonight... There's a little more leniency. Mandy, would you be willing to take a stroll down to the water with me? I'd love to see it in the moonlight."

Mandy nodded. She loved the waterfront, with the backdrop of colourful houses and the boats bobbing on the surface. She loved to see the moon reflected off the calm waters, and imagine mermaids and sea monsters.

All this she generally did alone. And now he wanted to spend more time with her. She glanced up at the clock. Midnight was somehow fast approaching. She had no idea what time the ball went on until, or whether Anya would be wanting to head home. But it was within easy walking distance, and she did not think her sister would mind her abandoning her.

"I'll just let my sister know, so she doesn't worry," she said, and disappeared back inside. The crowd had thinned out a little, but not by much. People were still dancing, although more and more of them were sitting drinking and chatting instead. Anya was sat in a corner with Tommy and several other cadets. Her sister's eyes lit up when she approached.

"I wondered where you'd disappeared to," she said, a suggestive tone in her voice.

Mandy rolled her eyes. "Just getting some fresh air. But I was going to go for a walk with Laurie. Just didn't want you to worry."

Anya grinned. "I won't worry. Are you coming home tonight?"

"Of course!" Mandy insisted, wishing Anya would keep her voice down a little. "But I don't know how late. Are you heading home?"

"Tommy's going to walk me back soon. Mum and Dad will be asleep anyway, but I'll tell them where you are if they wake up."

Mandy leant in and pressed a kiss to her sister's cheek. She felt like a princess tonight, shimmering in the limelight instead of hiding in the shadows, watching everyone else have fun.

"Thank you, Annie," she said.

"Have fun!" Anya replied, that twinkle still in her eyes.

Laurie was waiting for her by the front door. He held out his hand and she took it, her pulse racing. Never before had a night felt so full of promise.

CHAPTER ELEVEN

Isla and Luca – 2022

Luca's heart was racing as he lit the candle, and it took him two attempts to get the flame to catch the wick. This was silly. It was Isla. The woman he loved. And his question would surely not be a total surprise.

It was hard not to remember the last time he had asked this question. He had thought then that he would be with Jessie for the rest of his life. And he probably would have been, had cancer not torn her away from him.

But it was no good thinking like that. What ifs and sliding doors. He was in love with Isla, and she was here, in love with him. That was what he needed to focus on.

So why was he so nervous?

He supposed it was because he wasn't confident she would say yes.

He knew she loved him. He knew she wanted to be with him. But she had been burnt before, and she valued her independence. She had said no when he wanted her to move in with him. And this was a much bigger commitment...

But he wanted her to know that he wanted that commitment. That he wasn't going anywhere. That he wanted to spend the rest of his life with her, to live with her and run his business with her and to have children with her, when she was ready.

She would be home soon. She was working in the café that Lee Knight owned. When Isla had arrived in Dartmouth, she'd had no money and no job, and she had picked up work in both Luca's bookshop and the café of her cousin's wife's sister. She wasn't desperately trying to pay off debts any more, and she had started editing Beth's books, too – but it was hard to persuade her not to work so hard. She liked the stability of her income, she'd said, and he didn't want to argue with her. He just didn't want her to be run ragged, trying to keep up with so many jobs. She'd also learnt to drive in that time, which at least meant that she wasn't wasting time waiting around for buses. While she spent most nights at his flat, he wanted to make it every night that they spent together.

He glanced at the clock. It was almost six, and she would surely be back at any minute. He poured out two glasses of wine and stirred the risotto that was all ready to serve. Then he checked the pocket of his jeans to make sure the ring box was still in there, took a deep breath, and glanced back at the clock.

It was then that the front door opened. Luca took a deep breath, and forced his face to appear normal. He turned just as she was putting down her handbag on the sofa, a smile on her lips.

"What's this in aid of?" she asked, slipping off her shoes and padding over to press a kiss to his lips. He angled his hips so there was no way she would feel the ring box, and tried to look nonchalant when she pulled away.

"Just thought we deserved a nice evening together," he said, pulling out a chair for her. "How was work?"

"Busy, as usual," she said. "But it'll calm down soon.

How was the shop?"

"A coach load of tourists came in all at once," he said, moving to the open-plan kitchen to start dishing up. "So it was a bit wild, but lots of sales, so that was good."

"I got a postcard from Beth," Isla said, rummaging in her handbag. "The place they're staying in looks beautiful!"

"I didn't know anyone sent postcards anymore," Luca said with a smile, grating parmesan over the two bowls.

"Well, she is a writer," Isla said with a shrug. "You know she writes most of her first drafts by hand?"

"I've seen her scribbling in a notebook," Luca said, carrying the bowls over. "But it seems like so much work to type something you've already written!"

"She's the author," Beth said, sniffing at her plate. "This smells amazing, Luca. You do spoil me!"

"Got to keep you coming back somehow," Luca said.

"I think you know it's not only your cooking that keeps me coming back."

"I wanted to talk to you about that, actually," Luca said, deciding his nerves could not wait until the end of dinner.

Isla furrowed her brow.

"You want me to cook more?" she asked. While she was good at baking, she didn't tend to be home in time to cook the main meal, and Luca happily did so.

He shook his head. "No, not that. I wanted to revisit the topic of us living together."

Isla put down her fork. "Luca..." she said. "You know I love you. But I can't-"

"I know, you don't want everything to be mine, you don't want to live in the house I shared with Jessie..."

"It's more about the security, Luca. I just can't-"

"I understand. And I respect that. But I want to move forward, Isla. I love you, and I want to be with you forever. As equals, as partners. So I wanted to ask you-"

The confusion on her face was not ideal, but he pressed on anyway, pushing his chair out and going down on one knee. Her eyes widened as he fumbled in his pocket for the ring box.

"Isla. I want to share everything with you. My life, my home, my business. I love you, and I don't want to hold off starting our life together."

She gasped, and he saw tears in her eyes as he finally asked the question.

"Will you marry me?"

Silence hung in the air for far too long. Luca knelt on the floor, his knee going stiff, waiting, hoping, fearing. She looked at the ring, and at him, and she bit her lip, and then tears rolled down her cheeks.

"You are a wonderful man, Luca," she said, and his heart dropped.

They sounded like the words that preceded 'no'.

Awkwardly he got to his feet, the ring box still in his hand.

She reached up and took his other hand. "Luca," she said, her eyes wide and filled with emotion. "I want to say yes."

"Then do," he said hoarsely.

"I... I need to think," she said, squeezing his hand. "I love you, Luca."

"Then surely the answer is obvious?"

"It should be," she whispered. "But I lost everything before, with a man I thought I loved."

"I know. But if we're married, then everything is

split. If anything goes wrong for us – which I don't think it will – then you'll be protected."

She smiled, a sad smile that was marred by tears. "I just need some time to think, Luca. I need to make sure I make the right decision."

Her words were like a knife to his heart. He knew she'd been burnt before. Knew that she struggled to trust. But all he could hear was that she didn't want to marry him. The woman he was in love with, the woman who had broken down the walls around his heart after the death of his wife, didn't want to make that commitment to him.

"Just give me a bit of time," she said. "To think about it. Please?"

He nodded stiffly and sat back down. This would have been far less awkward if he'd waited until after dinner. Now the risotto he had made was cooling and congealing before them, and the champagne in the fridge was unnecessary.

"Luca..." she whispered, but he couldn't bring himself to look at her. "I don't want to hurt you. I just..."

"Need to be sure," he said, his voice bitter. "I understand. Let's eat, shall we?"

CHAPTER TWELVE

Beth and Caspian – 2022

"Well?" Caspian's nervous voice came through the closed bathroom door. Beth was ill, and nervous, but that didn't mean she planned to let him in the bathroom with her. That was a line they had never crossed.

She glanced down at the test. It was the third she had taken. Caspian had brought back several, and she had decided one wasn't enough.

She'd rifled through the instructions to find the section in English, and triple-checked the images that showed a positive, negative, or invalid test.

And once again, the test was negative.

Beth sat on the side of the bathtub and sighed. She ought to be relieved. But it was hard to feel positive emotions when she felt sick and clammy and like the room was spinning.

She opened the door to find a white-faced Caspian on the other side.

"It will all be okay," he said when he saw her face.

She shook her head. "They're negative, Caspian," she said, stumbling back to the bed. It was the longest she'd been out of it in days and she was feeling much worse for it. "All of them."

"Oh," he said, sitting on the edge of the bed. "Well,

that's good, isn't it?"

Beth nodded. "You know I don't want a baby right now. But it doesn't explain why I feel so awful..."

"No. No it does not. Beth, we need to get you to a doctor. Please?"

And it was a testament to how ill Beth felt that she did not argue.

◆ ◆ ◆

Caspian felt sick as he waited for the doctor to return. In the hospital bed, Beth seemed to look even more ill. She was paler than usual, there were dark circles under her eyes, and she had clearly lost weight in the week since she had become ill.

He ought to have brought her to a doctor earlier.

"Have you told Lee?" he asked, tapping his foot on the floor. He wished there was something he could do to help.

Beth shook her head. "No. I don't want to worry her."

"You don't want me to message now, then?"

"No," Beth said, her eyes widening. "She can't do anything, and she'll only stress. I'll let her know once they've got me fixed up."

The doctor, who thankfully spoke decent English, had asked lots of questions of both Beth and Caspian. Since Caspian had not been ill, he had ruled out several options, and with it going on for so long, it did not seem to be food-related. He had ordered blood tests, and a pregnancy test, although Caspian was confident that would be negative.

He needed them to find out what was wrong with her and fix it. Seeing her feeling so ill, and being unable to do anything to help her, terrified him. Without her, he was nothing.

"Stop looking so worried," Beth said, rolling onto her side with a wince. "We're in the right place now. It's probably something really obvious."

When the doctor finally returned, he was accompanied by a nurse with an IV bag and stand.

"Mrs Blackwell," the doctor said. "It seems you have contracted malaria. We must start your treatment immediately, before the disease progresses any further."

"Malaria?" Caspian said, frowning. "But I didn't think there was any malaria in Greece. We didn't have to take anti-malaria tablets..."

"It's rare," the doctor said, as the nurse switched out Beth's saline IV for the new medicine. "And so they are not routinely prescribed. But in the rural areas, it is possible to be bitten by malaria-carrying mosquitoes."

"The farm we visited," Caspian said, looking to Beth. There was fear in her eyes now, and it made his stomach flip. He reached out and took her hand.

"But these drugs, they will make her well again?"

"We have every reason to believe so, Mr Blackwell. Mrs Blackwell is young and healthy, and we've caught it in plenty of time."

Caspian nodded, his mouth feeling dry, and tried to give Beth a reassuring smile.

"We will keep Mrs Blackwell in hospital for a few days, while the treatment works," the doctor said.

"Should I be trying to get her home?" Caspian asked.

"I would highly recommend she begins treatment here. But once we discharge her, you may wish to return home to recuperate. Do you have insurance, to cover the costs of treatment here?"

Caspian nodded. Not that it mattered to him if he didn't. He would spend every penny he had and more on making sure she was well. But things would surely be simpler back at home. He knew nothing about malaria. The doctor didn't seem too concerned, just keen to get started on the treatment. But perhaps that was just his personality.

Once they were left alone once more, Beth asked for some water, and then for her phone.

"I guess I'd better tell Lee," she said. "Only I could catch malaria in somewhere like Greece."

"Being an author is a dangerous business," Caspian said with a half-smile. While he was relieved that an answer, and a treatment, had been found, he still felt in the dark about the prognosis. He liked to take charge, to know what he was dealing with and to get it sorted. But this wasn't his area of expertise. He needed to trust the doctors, no matter how hard it was to do so.

CHAPTER THIRTEEN

Mandy – 1983

The moon reflected on the water, sending a luminescent glow across the colourful houses on the opposite side of the bank. As they had walked down to the waterfront, they had chatted about their families, their homes, their childhoods. Mandy never wanted the night to end. The tingle in her arm where it was linked through his made her whole body feel electrified. The night seemed full of possibilities and excitement, and she could not remember ever feeling this way before.

"Where do you most want to visit?" Mandy asked as they strolled along.

"Everywhere," he said with a wide grin. "I love meeting new people, learning new languages... Although I would love to see America, which won't offer the new language. There are so many places in Europe I want to see. And then Japan..." He glanced down at her. "The list is pretty long."

"I'd love to see Paris," Mandy said, something she had never admitted before. Just because she didn't want to move away from her beloved Dartmouth, did not mean she was totally against seeing a little more of the world.

"Paris is beautiful," he said. "The most romantic city in the world."

He stopped and turned to face Mandy, and her stomach fluttered. "I wasn't even sure I was going to go to the ball tonight," he said.

"No?" Mandy said, her mouth dry and her heart racing. "Seems like a rite of passage!"

"I suppose so," he said, his dark eyes twinkling in the moonlight. "But I've never been one for dancing, and I thought it would be dull."

"And was it?"

"The very opposite of dull," he said. And then his hand moved to her cheek and he brushed a thumb against his cheek, anchoring his fingers in her hair at the nape of her neck. She tilted her head backwards and as he lowered his lips to hers, her eyes fluttered closed.

They were warm and full and she wrapped her arms around his neck, pulling him closer, her heart feeling like it might explode right out of her chest. She had been kissed before, but never like this. His tongue met hers and teeth clashed and the fire in her body raged wildly. How had she made it to twenty-one and never felt such a violent surge of emotions before?

When they pulled apart, her chest was heaving and her hair was almost certainly not in the perfect updo it had been in before. She smiled up at him, her heart glowing, and he touched his thumb to her lips.

"Tonight has been magical, Mandy," he said. "You know I'll be gone, for a while," he said, and her heart dropped a little. She nodded.

"But when I'm back-"

She reached up and touched a finger to his lips. "Let's not make promises we can't keep," she said. "If this is just tonight, then I'm still very pleased I came to the ball."

Without speaking, they began to walk again, back the way they came. But instead of heading off towards the naval college, they entered the little park. Mandy pointed out the beautiful old bandstand, with its black metal fencing and bright white wood panels. The moonlight illuminated it, and behind them, the tall stone fountain tinkled away.

"I bet this has seen a lot of romance over the years, too," Laurie said.

Mandy nodded. She'd always thought it was an extremely romantic spot. Not that she'd ever experienced any romance there.

Not until tonight.

He held out his hand. "Will you dance with me?"

Mandy blushed and giggled. "Here? There's no music!"

He began to hum, and it didn't take Mandy long to recognise the tune of 'The Winner Takes It All'. She took his hand, his touch setting her skin on fire once more, and they began to slowly sway to the music. Neither really knew what they were doing beyond some simple steps, but Mandy felt like a princess floating on a cloud. She had meant what she said. If this was just for tonight, then she would treasure it forever.

But if it could be more...

She blinked and focused on the tune he had continued to hum. They wanted entirely different lives. She would ruin this perfect moment if she let her mind wander to impossibilities.

She laid her head on his shoulder and felt him press a kiss to the top of her head. She had no idea how late it was. The ball was surely over by now. There were a few cars on the road, but she had no idea if one held her sister.

All she knew, all she could think about, was this moment, in the arms of Laurie Blackwell, her heart soaring and her pulse racing.

A night that would fill her dreams forever.

CHAPTER FOURTEEN

Lee and James – 2022

The message started with *'Don't panic'*, so of course the very first thing Lee did was panic.

She was sitting in the living room, feeding baby Harry, and watching the clock to make sure she wasn't late picking up Holly from school, when the message from her sister Beth came through. She was pleased to see her name pop up, since she hadn't been very communicative for the last week of her trip. Lee had assumed she was having fun, and she felt a little jealous. As happy as she was snuggling her baby boy, it was hard not to feel a twinge of longing when she saw photos of her sister's athletic body lying out in the Grecian sun.

Any jealousy was replaced with panic when she read the message, however.

Don't panic. I've somehow contracted malaria and am staying in hospital for a few nights. I've started treatment and we're going to come home as soon as I can. XX

Lee immediately typed a reply, deleted it, and typed another. Then she sighed, and hit dial. This was not a conversation to have over text message.

When the phone was eventually answered, it was

not by her little sister, but the deep tones of her brother-in-law, Caspian.

"Hey, Lee," he said, and she swore she heard anxiety in his voice. That only made her panic more. "Sorry, they're just checking Beth over again, she can't answer right now."

"Is she okay?" Lee asked, her voice a little shaky.

"She's been better," Caspian said. Lee could picture her sister watching him on the phone, telling him off for saying the wrong thing. "But they've got her on this treatment now, and they seem to think that will do the trick."

"Malaria can be really serious," Lee said, biting her lower lip. "I didn't even know you could catch it in Greece."

"Neither did we," Caspian said with a sigh.

"Do you need anything?" Lee asked. "Money? Stuff sent over? Planes booked?"

"We're sorted, thanks Lee," Caspian said.

"Well tell her I love her," Lee said. "And get her to give me a ring when she can."

"I will. She'll be okay, Lee. I'll make sure she is."

By the time the conversation had ended, it was very definitely time to leave to pick Holly up from school. But of course, baby Harry had fallen asleep at the end of his feed. Being a mother of two seemed to involve a lot of juggling to try and not leave anyone unhappy. James wouldn't be home for hours. She wanted his reassurance about Beth. She wished he worked more standard hours. At least then she would know she had the evenings to look forward to with him. But with the shifts he worked, she couldn't keep track week to week when he would be home, who was cooking, whether she had a whole weekend to fill without him for support.

And in the corner, her laptop gathered dust. She was a one-woman law firm, so while she was on maternity leave, her business stagnated. The café continued, under Gina's diligent care. In truth, Gina didn't really need Lee any more to make the business successful. But Lee didn't want to remove herself entirely from it. It had been her first tie to this place, the place that had made her jump out of her comfort zone and stay in this unique town that had captured her heart.

The town, the man, the people. She'd fallen in love with it all. And now she had her two beautiful children, and her sister lived nearby too. Well, when she wasn't swanning off catching tropical diseases.

She ought to be overjoyed every day, she thought. She could go back to law work once Harry was a bit older. There was no need to feel like she had lost a part of herself.

Once she had picked Holly up, and tried to find out how her day had gone (with the only information shared that they'd had pizza for lunch), Lee found herself not wanting to go home. She didn't want to sit and worry about Beth, with no one to talk to about her worries.

"How about a trip to see Nanny Mandy?" she asked, and this was met by cheers from Holly. Harry was sleeping happily in his car seat, and as long as Lee was there to feed him, she was sure he'd be content wherever they were.

Mandy wasn't really Holly's grandmother. She was Beth's mother-in-law, and Holly had two grandmothers of her own that she saw fairly regularly. But Mandy was very much a part of their lives, and so the nickname had arisen quite naturally. And today Lee wanted to be with someone who knew Beth, who would be able to reassure her that everything would be okay.

When she'd come to Devon, Lee's only relatives had been her mother and her sister. And with the hours she'd worked as a lawyer, she'd barely seen them.

But now she had a sprawling extended family that she knew she could rely on if she ever needed anything. She saw her own mother much more frequently, although they still had their issues. Her sister was around all the time, and they had reconciled with their father, and saw him and his husband as often as they could. Then there were James's parents, his brother and sister and their families, Beth's husband and his mum and cousin too. There was always someone to turn to.

She hoped Mandy wouldn't mind her turning up unannounced. It had been such a spur-of-the-moment decision, and by the time they were outside Mandy and Jonah's cottage, it wasn't even four in the afternoon.

By the time she had got the kids out of the car, Mandy had opened the front door and was beaming at them.

"Lee! And Holly, and Harry. What a delightful surprise!"

"Are you busy?" Lee asked with an apologetic smile.

"Not at all. And the kettle's just boiled. Come in, come in."

Holly ran up to her and gave her a hug, and as usual came away with a sweet in her little hand. She looked over to Lee who laughed. "Go on then. But no sticky marks on Nanny Mandy's sofa!"

Once Holly was happily playing with a box of Lego that Mandy kept around for her visits, and Harry was feeding yet again, Mandy mentioned Beth.

"I presume you've spoken to Beth?"

Lee shook her head. "Just Caspian."

"Don't worry too much, dear," Mandy said, reaching out and taking her hand. "They'll get her sorted."

Holly seemed to be engrossed in her play, but Lee was still careful with what she said. She didn't want her sensitive daughter being worried about her Auntie Beth.

"Caspian always seems so level-headed," she said, taking a sip of her tea. "I'm glad they're together."

"He is," Mandy said. "And Beth is, too."

Lee nodded. She often still thought of her sister as the flighty twenty-year-old she had been for so many years. But in truth, Mandy was right. Beth had matured so much in the years since she had moved to Devon, and even without Caspian, she would have handled this crisis.

Even so, Lee was glad she didn't have to handle it alone.

The front door clicked open, and Mandy glanced towards it. "Jonah?" she called.

"No, it's Isla," a voice came back. She appeared in the living room, and smiled when she saw Lee. "Didn't realise you had company, sorry."

"I turned up unannounced," Lee said with an apologetic smile. "Were you at the café today?"

"I was. All going well, nice and busy," she said, waving at Holly who had looked up from her Lego for a moment.

"That's what I like to hear," Lee said.

"Did you stay here last night, dear?" Mandy asked. "I thought I heard you come back late."

"Sorry, didn't mean to wake you."

"You didn't, just checking everything is okay. I wasn't expecting you home."

Isla sighed, and took a seat opposite them both.

"I'm not sure it is," she said. "But I don't know..."

"Has something happened?" Mandy asked, concern colouring her tone.

"I should go," Lee said, drinking her hot cup of tea as quickly as she could. She didn't want to intrude on a real family moment.

"You don't have to go anywhere," Mandy said.

"No, you don't," Isla agreed. "In fact, I could probably use your advice."

CHAPTER FIFTEEN

Isla – 2022

Lego bricks clicked in the background as Lee and Aunt Mandy waited for her to reveal why she needed their advice. Isla's stomach was churning. It had been since that awkward meal last night, since she had hurt Luca so thoroughly, since she had made up some lie about needing to get home because she just couldn't stay there with him looking like that.

She took a deep breath, twisting her fingers together in her lap. "Luca asked me to marry him."

There was a gasp from Aunt Mandy.

"Surely that's wonderful news, dear?" Aunt Mandy asked.

"If you'd said yes, I presume you wouldn't be here, looking like you're about to throw up," Lee said.

Isla nodded and pursed her lips. "I couldn't," she said in a half-whisper.

"Why not?" Aunt Mandy asked, leaning forwards. "You love him, don't you?"

Isla let out a strangled half-sob. "I do," she said. "But I thought I loved Toby too."

"I think Luca is an entirely different kettle of fish to Toby," Aunt Mandy said.

"So do I," Isla admitted. "But when things ended

with Toby, I lost everything. I don't think I can go through that again. A broken heart and a broken life..."

"But if you marry Luca, then you wouldn't be in that situation, would you," Lee said. "Look, forgive me for being blunt. It's the lawyer in me. But if things did go wrong with Luca, you'd be entitled to half of everything. It's far more secure than just dating or living together."

"That's what Luca says," Isla said with a sad smile.

"He's a sensible man," Lee said.

"It won't protect me from a broken heart though, will it."

Aunt Mandy leant forward and took her hand, a knowledgeable smile on her lips. "Nothing can do that, sweetheart. But Luca loves you, and you love him. And it seems he wants you to feel safe."

Isla nodded, a tear coming to her eye. "I think he does. He wants us to buy a house, together. Get a mortgage, settle down, make everything official."

"I don't think he's looking for an easy escape, then," Aunt Mandy said.

"I agree with Mandy, if my opinion is useful at all," Lee said.

"It definitely is," Isla said, wiping her eyes with her sleeve. "I feel like I was stupid to not say yes now."

"Not stupid," Lee said. "Cautious. You've been burnt before. Luca will understand. James has certainly understood when my jealousy has got the better of me, thanks to my cheater of an ex-husband."

Mandy nodded. "And Jonah understood why it took me so long to agree to date him. Why it wasn't easy for me to marry again, even so long after losing my Laurie."

"He looked so hurt though," Isla said. "Like he'd put himself out there and I had just shot him down." She dug her fingernails into her palms. "Which is exactly what I did. Oh, god, what if he doesn't want to marry me any more? What if he's returned the ring? What if-"

Aunt Mandy put a hand on her knee. "Isla. Calm down. If a man buys a ring and proposes, he is not going to change his mind that quickly. Tell him all of this. Tell him you were wrong. If he's the man I think he is, he won't want to lose you over this."

◆ ◆ ◆

Isla was exhausted from a hard day at the café, but she couldn't sit still. Not when she'd hurt Luca so badly. Why hadn't she just said yes? He knew why she was cautious, and had tried to mitigate it in his proposal. Like her Aunt Mandy, Luca had lost his spouse, and had not dated for years. And then he and Isla had fallen for one another, and now he was proposing marriage.

How difficult had it been for him to ask her to marry him, after losing his first, much-loved wife?

Isla wandered the waterfront in Dartmouth, needing to gather her thoughts before she went up to see Luca. He hadn't been in touch all day. Would he refuse to see her? Her mind swirled as she watched a small boat crossing the water. She hadn't ever taken the ferry across. She knew her cousin's wife, Beth, had worked over at Greenway, Agatha Christie's old home, when she had first moved to Devon. But Isla had never had a reason, and now never had the time, to visit it.

She wanted to redo the previous night. To hear his words of love and to not feel panic surging through her. To tell him that she loved him, and that she would be delighted to marry him.

Because Lee was right. Luca was offering her

security along with his declarations of love. She wanted to live with him, and yet she couldn't stop herself from worrying about everything falling apart.

On her way up to Luca's flat, she paused to look in the window of an estate agents. In the centre were two massive homes, each worth over a million. Homes she could never even dream of living in. But around them were more reasonable options, and hope blossomed in her chest. She had never had a home she could call her own. She had lived with her mother, then in flatshares, then with Toby. And when everything had fallen apart, she had moved in with Aunt Mandy, and begun to split her time between Aunt Mandy's and Luca's after they had begun to date.

But to have somewhere that was her home, hers and Luca's...

She made a note of two of the houses, and started off up the hill. If only Luca would see her, she would endeavour to show him that he had not been wrong to ask her to share his life.

CHAPTER SIXTEEN

Mandy – 1983

Time slipped by as though in a dream. They talked, laughed, kissed and danced, never mentioning that soon they would have to go back to their separate lives. At one point, Mandy shivered and Laurie shrugged off his smart double-breasted jacket and put it around her shoulders. It was warm and smelled of his cologne and the gesture warmed her heart as well as her body.

She had never stayed out all night with a man before. She had never done anything with a man before. He never suggested anything more than kissing though, and she was relieved. She didn't want to spoil the night with fears or admissions or refusals. And anyway, where would they go? He was a naval cadet. She lived with her parents. This one magical night was all they could ever have, and she didn't want anything to ruin it.

"I think the sun is coming up," Mandy said, pointing over to where the sky was beginning to lighten across the water. She didn't wear a watch, and so she had no idea what time it was, but she was sure dawn was approaching. Her voice was beginning to fade a little, after so long talking, but nothing could make her want to end this night.

He sighed and turned to face her. "I think you're

right. I will have to get back to the academy soon..."

She nodded. She would have to be home before her parents woke up. Otherwise there would be too many questions. Besides, she was supposed to be working today – although she didn't know how she would have the energy after a whole night of no sleep. Perhaps she would pretend to be ill.

"Will you dance with me?" he asked. "Once more, before I go?"

She nodded. It didn't feel silly any more. Not when they had twirled around the bandstand together several times, giggling and kissing and tripping over each other's feet.

This time, she began to hum, and he joined her, their voices mingling together as their bodies pressed close, savouring this last moment. She knew, no matter where her life took her, that when she heard Endless Love she would think of Laurie Blackwell, and this night that had shown her what life could offer.

The sun began to rise in the east, and as it did he pressed his lips fervently against hers, and she responded with a similar sense of desperation and longing.

They pulled away and pressed their foreheads together, each savouring the moment. Mandy caught sight of the large watch on his wrist. It was just after six. She needed to get home, and she was sure he did too.

"I'll walk you back," he said.

Mandy shook her head. "I don't want you to get in trouble if you're not back. Besides, I only live over there."

She pointed in the vague direction of the shop and their little home above it.

"I will see you again, Mandy," he said, and the kiss he pressed to her lips this time was brief but heartfelt. "I promise."

"Thank you for a wonderful evening," she said, removing his jacket and handing it back to him. The early morning air was cool against her bare shoulders, and she looked forward to slipping into bed and catching up on some sleep. "Goodbye, Laurie."

She watched him walk away for far too long before coming to her senses and walking as fast as she could in her heels back home. It wasn't that she would be in trouble for being home so late, but that she would have to answer all of their questions. And she didn't have any answers. Nothing had happened, really. They didn't need to worry.

And yet she'd had the best night of her life.

The building was still silent, although she knew it wouldn't be for long. Mum and Dad never slept much past half six in the morning. There was too much to be done before the shop opened.

Thinking she ought to let Anya know she was home, she slipped into her sister's bedroom and tapped on her shoulder. Anya's make-up was still on her face and her hair was splayed out over the pillow, in clear need of a good brush. When she opened her eyes, they were rather bleary, and she wondered whether her sister had overindulged in the champagne at the ball. Either that or a lack of sleep. Mandy was sure she would be feeling the same, once she had actually been to sleep.

When her sister saw who had woken her, a sleepy smile spread across her face.

"What time is it?" she asked groggily.

"Just after six," Mandy said, careful to keep her voice low. "Mum and Dad will be up soon, but I need to go to bed."

"Did you have a good night?" Anya asked, propping herself up on her elbows and blinking away sleep.

Mandy couldn't help but smile. "Yeah," she said. "Did you?"

"Not as exciting as yours, by the looks of it," she said with a snort. "But yeah, not bad."

Mandy stifled a yawn.

"Go to bed," Anya said. "Mum and Dad left a note that they would open up. So you don't need to set an alarm."

Relief washed through Mandy's body. "Thanks."

"But I'll expect every detail tomorrow afternoon!" she said, as Mandy made her exit. She closed the door as quietly as she could and slipped into her room. It took a few moments to divest herself of the gown and the heels, as well as the tight underwear that was feeling like a vice after so many hours of wearing it. Then she pulled her old, comfortable nightie over her head and climbed into bed, her body relaxing into the mattress in relief. It had been a wonderful night, but it had also involved a lot of walking, talking and being out in the cold night air, and her body was very keen for a rest. As her eyes fluttered closed, her mind replaying the events of the evening, she heard her parents starting their day. Blissful sleep washed over her, and she dreamt magical dreams of dancing and the moonlight and Laurie.

CHAPTER SEVENTEEN

Beth and Caspian – 2022

Caspian felt an overwhelming sense of relief as the plane took off, leaving Greece below them. Beth was wrapped in a blanket beside him, looking pale and thin, but free from the wires and tubes of the hospital.

She would need time to convalesce. She would need to see a doctor in the UK, be prescribed any ongoing treatment, and take it easy for a while. But she was out of the woods, and Caspian couldn't wait to get home with her.

After she had been diagnosed with malaria, he had made the mistake of looking it up online, and realised just how severe it could be. He'd spent the week she was in the hospital sleeping on a chair beside her, having nightmares about losing her.

He would be very grateful to sleep in his own bed, with his wife beside him, with the worries of this trip behind them. Never before had he been so pleased to leave a holiday destination.

"Are you comfortable?" he asked, and Beth looked over to him and smiled.

"I'm fine, Caspian. You don't need to keep worrying

about me."

He took hold of her hand. "I can't avoid that, I'm afraid."

She reached up and put her palm to his cheek. "You look exhausted."

"It's not been the most relaxing trip," he said, turning his head to press a kiss to a palm.

"I'm sorry."

"I don't think catching malaria was your fault, Beth."

"I wanted to go out to that farm."

"We didn't know," he said with a shrug. "All's well that ends well."

"Is your mum picking us up?" she asked, leaning her head against his shoulder with a yawn.

"Lee is," he said. "She insisted. I told her mum could do it."

"There's no changing Lee's mind when she wants something," Beth said, and he could hear the smile in her voice. "She sounded pretty worried on the phone. It'll be good to see her."

"Will she have told your parents?"

"I doubt it," Beth said, stretching her legs in front of her. "Mum gets stressed and would undoubtedly have rung me to ask why on earth I had decided to catch malaria. And dad... We tend to only tell him the good news."

"Would he not want to know?" Caspian murmured into her hair.

Beth shrugged. "There were so many years he wasn't around," she said. "I know now that he wasn't totally at fault, but I guess it's hard to change the habit of dealing with things by myself."

"Well, not totally by yourself," Caspian said. "You know you've always got me. And Lee, and Mum, and Isla, and-"

Beth giggled. "Yes, quite a family now. I'll ring Mum and Dad once we're home, fill them both in. I can deal with Mum's stress or Dad just turning up now I feel a bit more human."

◆ ◆ ◆

Caspian did everything once they touched down. Carried the bags, got them through the special assistance line at passport control, and sat her down to wait while he collected the rest of their luggage. Normally she would have argued that she was perfectly capable, but she didn't have the energy. The flight had drained her, although she didn't want to admit it to Caspian. He had looked so worried for so long, and she didn't want to add to his troubles. All she wanted was to get home and climb into her own bed for a long sleep.

Lee was waiting outside in the pick-up area, and jumped out of her car the second she saw them. She pulled Beth into a hug, while Caspian dealt with the luggage, and it was a long time before she let go.

"It's so good to see you," she whispered, and Beth hugged her back tightly even though she was feeling a little shaky at standing for so long.

"You too, sis," she said, and when they parted she could see her sister's eyes were watery.

"You scared me," Lee said.

"Scared myself a bit," Beth admitted. "And Caspian."

"Let's get you sat down," Caspian said, and Lee wiped her eyes and let Caspian help Beth into the car.

"No kids?" Beth said once they were all strapped in.

"I thought Holly's excitement over seeing Auntie Beth might be a bit much if you were feeling rough," Lee said. "James is off, so I left them both with him."

Beth smiled. Whilst she adored her niece and nephew, Lee was right. It wouldn't have been easy to keep up the conversation that Holly would have demanded when her head still felt fuzzy.

"Was it a good trip?" Lee asked as she drove. "Before the malaria?"

"Yeah, it was," Beth said, taking Caspian's hand and squeezing it.

"It was beautiful," he said. "But I'm not sure I'll remember anything from it except the hospital stay."

"Oh, don't say that," Beth said with a sigh. "I'm still going to write that book, once I feel better. And there won't be a mention of malaria in it. We can't let the bad outweigh the good."

Caspian squeezed her hand and smiled. "I'll try to be as positive as you, my love."

"Everyone wants to see you," Lee said as they made their way towards the village of Strete, where Caspian and Beth lived. "But I've put them off for today."

"Maybe a bit longer than just today," Caspian said, with a wary look at Beth.

"Well, your mum will want to come round," Beth said. "I think I can manage that. But maybe we'll hold off on everyone else, for a few days."

"I think Caspian will be an effective bouncer," Lee said with a laugh. "And I will keep the kids away until you've got some energy back, don't worry. It's just wonderful to see you up and about."

"It's good to be home," Beth said, grinning as she caught sight of the sea in the distance. The ocean in

Greece just wasn't the same. This was home, and her heart felt full of joy at returning.

CHAPTER EIGHTEEN

Lee and James – 2022

Lee did not wait around once she had seen that Beth was settled in bed. She knew her sister well, and although she did not say it, she could tell she wanted to rest alone.

As she drove home, finding it odd to be alone in the car, relief spread through her chest. While she would never have admitted it out loud, she had been concerned for Beth's health. She had researched malaria, and knew the dangers when it was not caught early. And what constituted early? There had been no preventatives, and she had been ill enough to need a stay in a foreign hospital. Lee's mind had gone wild with the possibilities. She had even looked into flights to Greece for herself, if she needed to go out and be with her sister.

But it finally seemed like all was well. Beth was home, tired and thin and a need of recuperation, but home safe. Life could be so unpredictable. One moment, Beth was living the life she had dreamt of, travelling and researching with the love of her life. And the next she was in hospital, scared and unsure of what the future held. It was a lesson, surely, to not take anything for granted.

For so many years, Lee had taken her life for granted. She had loved her work, put everything into it, but she had not thought about anything beyond it. She had not realised her marriage was falling apart. She had not realised that she had nothing and no one to rely on. And now she did. Now she had everything she had dreamed of. A husband who was devoted to her. Children she adored. And a career she had built herself that was waiting for her.

But did it have to wait? Was there no way that she could have it all? Her time with her children, and the career that she loved? She thought they could afford it. They were financially secure, after all. And her law work brought in more money than the café or even James's police work.

What would James think, she thought to herself, as she pulled off the road down the narrow lane that led to their picturesque cottage. They barely saw each other as it was. How would he feel about her going back to work before Harry was even one?

It was surely worth the conversation at least.

She felt nervous as she put her key into the lock, although she did not fully understand why. She and James had a good marriage, she knew that. Yes, of late there had been a little more sniping than usual, with James being stressed at work, and Lee feeling frustrated and missing her own work. Not to mention the lack of sleep. But surely that was all pretty standard for a couple with a newborn baby? She tried to remember back to the time after Holly had been born. Their relationship had been much newer than. The pregnancy had been such a surprise that their supposedly casual dating had turned into something much more serious very quickly.

But among the glow of finally being a mother, of that much longed-for baby, and James asking her to marry him, she did remember some struggles in those early days.

Well, she was going to raise it today. It was surely better to talk about these things than to leave them to fester. When she entered the living room, she could not help but smile at the image that met her. Harry was asleep in his father's arms, and Holly sat beside them both, making James read a treasured book for the five hundredth time, and often being reminded to keep her voice down so as not to wake her baby brother.

When they heard her enter, they both looked up. Holly jumped off the sofa and ran to her, hugging her as though she had not seen her in days, rather than just a few hours. James smiled and took the opportunity to close the book.

"How's Beth?" he asked.

"Much better than she was, I think. She'll need to rest, but it's a relief that she is home."

"A relief for all of us. You didn't have to rush back – I'm fine with these two. My parents asked if they could pop over and take them to the park." Holly cheered at the word park and was promptly shushed by both her parents. Harry squirmed a little in his father's arms but stayed asleep nonetheless.

"That sounds perfect," Lee said. She wanted to have an honest conversation with James, and it would be far easier to do so without the interruptions of two small children. James's parents loved spending time with their grandchildren and Lee loved the bond that they had. She never had much of a relationship with any grandparents herself, and she was thrilled that her children had this opportunity.

An hour later, with steaming mugs of coffee and an unusually quiet house, Lee settled on the sofa beside her husband.

"Well, this is rare," he said with a smile on his face. "Both at home and the house to ourselves. What should we do?"

There was a suggestive tone to his words that made Lee grin. "Would sleep be the wrong answer?" she asked.

He laughed. "No, probably not!"

"I actually wanted to talk, first," Lee said, crossing her legs on the sofa.

"Oh?" James said, raising his eyebrows. "That sounds rather ominous!"

"I hope not," Lee said, biting her lower lip. "I don't want you to think I'm unhappy, or ungrateful, or-"

"I promise not to think anything bad if you spit it out, Lee. You're making me anxious here."

She tried to smile. "You don't need to be," she said. "I love you, James."

"I love you too," he said. He ran a hand through his blond hair as he waited for her to say more.

"I love you, I love this house, I love our children, I love our life," she said.

"That's good..." he said, looking confused. "I do too, of course."

"But I miss my work, James. I don't feel like myself if I'm not working. And I don't want to feel irritated or frustrated with you, or the children, but I would like to take up some law work again. Just for a couple of days a week..."

"Okay," James said. "That doesn't sound unreasonable."

Lee smiled and her stomach untwisted a little. "It doesn't? We can afford childcare, or we can ask one of our many relatives. I can pump, so he can still have breast milk, and feed when I'm around. I know we barely see each other, and-"

"Lee," James said, reaching out and putting a hand on her knee. "I am on board. You don't need to get stressed about this.

"You don't think I'm a terrible mother? Wanting to go back to work when my baby isn't even six months old?"

"You are very far from being a terrible mother," James said. "You don't have to forget who you are entirely in order to be an amazing parent. And we can definitely make this work."

Lee leant over and pressed a kiss to his lips. She could taste the coffee they had both been drinking. "Thank you," she murmured.

"There's nothing to thank me for," he said. "We're in this together, we make decisions that will make us all happy. And on that note..."

Lee pulled back slightly and appraised his expression. Did he look slightly nervous himself?

"What would you think about not going with a nursery or one of our relatives to look after Harry?"

"I don't understand," Lee began.

"I hate how little I see you, and the kids. And I think we could afford it if I went part-time, or even... took a sabbatical for a while. Took care of the kids. I'm not finding work very fulfilling at the minute, and the thought of missing out on everything with you three while I'm not happy at work-"

"I think it's a great idea," Lee said, keen for him to know that she supported him just as much as he supported her. "Either part-time, or the sabbatical. With the income from my law work, we can definitely make it work, however you want to do it."

"You won't mind me being a house husband?"

She laughed at the ridiculous outdated term. "I love watching you with our children. I am definitely happier when you cook. And I would be ecstatic to get to see you more than I currently do."

James beamed. "I'll talk with work then, and we'll make a plan?"

"You know I love to make a plan," Lee said, unable to resist leaning in for another kiss.

"We've still got time for that nap," James said, glancing up at the clock. "They'll be out for a while yet."

"A nap sounds good," Lee said, running her hand through his soft blonde hair and pressing a kiss to his neck. "Are you going to join me?"

James pulled her into his lap and she giggled. Desire filled his eyes and Lee's heart felt light and full of joy.

"That's an invitation I will certainly not refuse, Mrs Knight."

CHAPTER NINETEEN

Isla and Luca – 2022

Luca loved the view of the boats from his flat. It had been one of the reasons he had bought it, along with his wife Jessie, when they had married. They both loved Dartmouth, loved to be able to look out over the town and see the people coming and going, and especially the boats.

When he had proposed to Isla, he had known it would mean leaving this place. She wanted stability, and perhaps she was right that they should start over somewhere new, that wasn't filled with his memories with Jessie – both the good and the very, very bad.

But Isla had not said yes to his proposal. She had gone home, and he had not seen her all day. He couldn't face messaging her, for it felt desperate to chase after a woman who had rejected him. She had his heart, but she didn't want to share his life, his name, his home. There didn't seem any way of moving past that pain. He wanted to be with her, but he wanted to move forwards, too. After Jessie, he had not thought he would ever marry again, and yet Isla had changed everything.

Would he now be alone with a broken heart once again?

It had been a long day in the bookshop, alone. It had rained, and that had driven people inside looking for shelter, and many of them had ended up purchasing something. But it was good to keep busy. He didn't want to dwell on the misery in his heart.

Would he see Isla that evening? They had not discussed their plans. The evening had ended awkwardly after that proposal. If he didn't see her, he would have to reach out the following day, and figure out where they were heading. He didn't like to let things fester, but it was hard to get over the rejection and face the possibility that they didn't have a future. He wanted to be with her, but how could they move forward if she didn't trust him, didn't want to share his life? He didn't want to spend forever in this limbo, spending most nights together but not officially living together. He wanted to move forward. And he had hoped she wanted to move forward with him.

He glanced over to the pictures on his wall. He had kept up pictures of Jessie, because she was part of him, part of his life, part of his history. And then there were photos of him and Isla. He had thought she was his future, and his heart broke at the idea that she might not be.

When he looked back out of the window, he saw Isla walking determinedly up the hill. Thankfully the evening was dry, and although she wore a coat, she didn't have the hood up. Her jaw was set and her hair pulled back. Was she coming here to tell him that things were over between them? Or did she have some suggestion of how they could move forward?

His stomach churned as she disappeared from view and he waited for her to come up. She had a key, but he did not know if she would use it in these circumstances.

Footsteps on the stairs, and he remained looking out to sea, awaiting his fate.

And then there was a tentative knock on the door. He rose, steeling himself to see her, trying to keep his mind clear and apathetic and accepting of whatever she had to say.

He opened the door and felt a wrench in his heart at the sight of her. She smiled, but it was not the usual beam that he could not help but return.

"Hi," she said, her voice a little hoarse.

"Hi."

"Can I come in?" she asked.

He stood aside and let her pass. Things felt oddly formal between them. He wanted to reach out and take her hand but something prevented him from doing so. He needed to know what she had to say first, before he let down his guard. He didn't know if he could cope with being so thoroughly rejected again.

"I messaged," she said. "I was worried..."

"Sorry," he said, avoiding her eyes. "It's been a busy day."

She nodded and visibly swallowed. "I understand."

"Would you like a drink?"

"Okay."

"Tea? Coffee? Wine?"

She paused for a moment, and he saw her glance at the clock.

"I don't think it's too early for wine," she said with a half-smile.

He nodded and disappeared into the kitchen, returning with an open bottle of red and two glasses. Silence filled the flat as he poured the wine, and he wondered if he ought to ask her outright where they went from here.

◆ ◆ ◆

He couldn't even look at her. It made Isla's heart ache to know that the man she loved was in so much pain because of her. She said yes to the drink to give her a moment to gather her thoughts. As he poured, she pulled out her phone, and pulled up one of the listings she had been looking at in the estate agent's window.

Luca picked up his glass of wine and raised it to his lips. He didn't seem to have anything to say to her, and she couldn't blame him. He had asked her to share his life, and she had responded less than enthusiastically.

But she had been wrong. She knew that now. He was the man she wanted to spend her life with – and he had done everything in order to make sure she felt safe and secure in a way that no one ever had done before.

Now she needed to persuade him that she was worth it.

"Luca," she said, and his eyes met hers. "I'm sorry."

He looked away. "It's fine, Isla. If you don't want-"

"But I do," she said. "I was scared, and I thought I needed time. But I don't need time."

He looked back at her, his eyes widening. "You don't?"

Isla shook her head. "I never want to end up in the position that Toby put me in again. And the fear of that made me too scared to say yes."

"But that's just it," Luca said, putting down his glass of wine and taking one of her hands in his. "I want to marry you so you don't have to worry about that. So that we can live our lives together and you know you are safe. Not just because I promise that will never happen, but because it legally cannot."

"I know," Isla said, her voice a little breathy. "I've been a stupid fool, Luca." She sniffed and held out her phone to him. "I want it all," she said. "The marriage, the shared business, the house together. I looked at some options..."

He glanced down at the phone fleetingly. "You're sure? I don't want you to feel like you have to say yes. But Isla, I love you. I want us to have a life together. A life where you're not staying away a night a week so that you feel safe."

"I want that too, Luca," she said, tears pooling in her eyes. She shoved the phone in her back pocket, and took both his hands in hers. "I thought I knew what love was. But I didn't. Not until I met you. When you asked me to marry you I should have said yes without thinking."

Luca shook his head. "No. You shouldn't have done. You've been hurt, and you didn't want to be hurt again. I should have understood that. You asked for time – it wasn't unreasonable."

"But I hurt you," Isla said, reaching up to cup his face. "And I never meant to do that."

"I know that now," he said, a tear in his eye. "I never thought I would ask another woman to marry me. So when I knew I wanted to marry you... It was a revelation. And when you said no..."

"I didn't say no," Isla said gently. "I am very definitely not saying no."

She took a deep breath and lowered herself down to one knee, keeping hold of his hands and looking up at him from the floor. "Luca, will you marry me?"

Luca dropped to the floor in front of her and gripped her hands tightly. "There's nothing I want more."

He dropped her hands then and wrapped them around her waist, pulling her closer, pressing his lips to hers. Her hands moved to his hair, gripping onto him, making sure that this was real, that he was real, that she was really going to marry this man that she loved so very much.

When they pulled apart, breathless and rather more ragged-looking than before, Luca grinned at her, his eyes a little glassy still.

"The ring," he said, jumping up. "You must have-"

Isla blinked away her tears of happiness as he reappeared with the black box that had caused so much drama the night before. When he clicked it open, she gasped. It was a beautiful square diamond, set on a rose-gold band.

"It's vintage," Luca said. "I saw it and immediately thought of you. If you don't like it-"

"I love it," Isla said, holding out her hand for him to slide it on. She was pleasantly surprised when it fit perfectly, and she held it up to the dying sunlight through the window to get a better look.

"Do you having any wine in? Or some champagne hidden away?" she asked with a grin. "Because this feels like a moment worthy of toasting."

CHAPTER TWENTY

Mandy – 1983-1984

A month after the most magical night of Mandy's life, and everything seemed so very different - and completely the same.

Every day, she got up and worked in the shop her parents owned, except for her day off, which she spent practising her sewing, or walking on the beach, or with her mother, redecorating Anya's bedroom now that she had left.

Nothing had changed about Mandy's plan or her day-to-day life, and yet she felt entirely different. Anya had left for university, as she had always planned to do. And Mandy missed her terribly. The house seemed empty without her, and without her sister and their friends to spend time off with, everything felt a little... meaningless.

It was nothing to do with Laurie Blackwell. Mandy told herself that sternly every time her mind wandered to the handsome naval cadet. She had always known that it was only going to be one magical night. He was the most handsome man she had ever met, and she was sure that while he was away from Dartmouth, he would meet some other girl. And then, when he was travelling the world, there would be plenty of girls to catch his eye.

Still, she knew when the cadets were due back into Dartmouth, knew that after Christmas there was a chance she would see Laurie again. She tried in vain not to care, but although she was sad when Anya returned to university after Christmas, there was part of her that knew Laurie was now back in Dartmouth. That there was a chance she might see him again.

He didn't know exactly where she lived, and they had not exchanged telephone numbers. She supposed he didn't have a permanent one, anyway. But she believed in fate, and if Laurie and she were going to meet again, she believed it would happen without prior organisation.

Besides, Dartmouth was a small town. Surely the odds were that they would run into each other at some point.

She looked out for him wherever she went. When she went out shopping with her mother, or out strolling across the beach, or walking up to the haberdashery for more sewing supplies. Her heart raced if she ever saw a man in naval uniform. But it was never him.

And then, on February fourteenth, a day filled with love and hearts and chocolates and hopes, she decided to go and sit in the old bandstand, on a whim. She wanted to feel some romance, or the memory of it at least, even if there was none left in her life. The day was cool but bright, and she walked briskly towards the park, and passed the fountain.

She stopped dead in her tracks at the sight that greeted her. She blinked a few times, sure that she was conjuring up an image of what she wanted to happen, rather than of reality.

But then the heart-stoppingly handsome naval cadet smiled broadly, took off his cap, and walked towards her.

Her pulse raced, her mouth went dry, and she groped around for something to say. Had she not thought about this meeting a hundred times? No matter how many times she told herself it would not happen, she had certainly imagined it.

"I didn't think I'd see you again," he said, and his voice was as rich and deep as she remembered, and his eyes just as intense.

"Neither did I," she said, her voice a little hoarse. She couldn't tell him that she had imagined this moment, that she had longed for it, despite believing it would never happen. That was far too embarrassing to admit.

"I should have asked exactly where you lived," Laurie said, running a hand through his dark hair. "I hoped you would come down here again at some point. At some point when I was down here too. My only other plan was to knock on every door in the town asking for you, but I haven't got that desperate. Yet."

Mandy felt breathless. He was here, before her, and he had wanted to find her. Considered asking at every door in town just to know where she lived.

"I didn't know if you would want to see me again," she admitted, for of course she had known where he was. There was only one place in town he could be.

He took a step forward, closing the gap between them. "I said I did, didn't I?"

Mandy nodded. "Yes. But I thought maybe that was just one of those things that you said. To be polite."

Laurie shook his head. "I wasn't being polite. I'm in town for a few months, before I have to go away again."

Mandy nodded, waiting for him to continue. She felt like she could breathe again. Like she had been living her life in black-and-white, and suddenly colour had burst back onto the scene. One evening with one man surely should not have such a profound effect, and yet she had to admit, at least to herself, that it had.

"I don't get much time off," he said, his eyes scanning her face, landing on her lips for a moment. "But perhaps I could take you out to dinner on Friday night?"

Mandy could not control the smile that spread across her face. "I'd like that very much."

Laurie leant in and pressed a brief kiss to her cheek. He smelled of soap, and a different aftershave than the one he had worn on the night of the ball. Mandy felt her cheeks blushing bright red.

"You better give me your address then, so I can pick you up. Don't want to have to knock on every door in the whole town now, do I."

◆ ◆ ◆

The dress she wore for the date with Laurie was the first garment she had made entirely herself. She checked the fit over and over, sure that there would be something wrong with it. It was a blue wrap dress, with blue ribbon around the waist. Nothing fancy, but it fit her perfectly, since it was made for her, and made her feel like she was floating.

Knowing that her parents were likely to meet Laurie that evening when he picked her up, she thought she'd better give them some warning.

"That's a nice dress, love," Mum said when she came into the living room. Their day had only just ended, and they always liked to sit with a cup of tea together before getting on with making dinner.

Mandy beamed. "Thank you. I made it." She was a

little shy to admit it, but was gratified by her parents' wide-eyed reaction.

"I didn't know you could sew like that," Mum said.

"I'll bring you my shirts next time, when there's a missing button," Dad said. "Your mum never sews them on straight!"

Mum tapped his arm good-naturedly and laughed. "It is a task I would happily delegate."

Nerves twisted in Mandy's stomach. Would he show up? Would their evening be as amazing as the night of the ball? There had been something special in the air that night, and she worried that it wouldn't be replicated.

"Are you going somewhere nice?" Dad asked.

"Yes," she said, her teeth catching her lower lip. "I'm going on a date."

The reaction once again was surprise, but that wasn't so gratifying. Had her life been so staid that her parents were shocked at her going on a date at nearly twenty-two years old?

Yes, it had been. That was the truthful answer, even if it wasn't something she wanted to admit.

"Anyone we know?" Mum asked, clearly trying to sound less interested than she was.

"He's a naval cadet," Mandy said. "I met him at that ball, with Anya."

"You can invite him in for a drink if you want, you know," Mum said.

Mandy shook her head. "We've got to get to the restaurant in time for the table," she said. She loved her parents but whatever this magical phenomenon was with Laurie, it would certainly be brought back down to earth after an interrogation from her mother. If things continued between them... But no. She was getting ahead of herself. He would be leaving again soon. She needed to learn to live in the moment.

She waited outside for him, since it was dry, and her heart leapt when she spotted him walking up the hill.

"Are you keeping me a secret from your parents?" he asked. It was the first time she had seen him without his uniform on, in dark trousers and a light blue jumper. He looked different, but no less handsome. If she had thought the uniform was what made her head so giddy around him then she was clearly mistaken.

"No, of course not," she said with a giggle. "But I don't think we'll make it to the restaurant before it closes if they get talking."

"Fair enough," he said, offering her his arm. "You look very pretty."

Mandy was pleased that dusk had fallen and that her flaming red cheeks surely wouldn't be as noticeable. "Thank you," she murmured as they made their way down the hill towards the centre of town. She didn't know where he had picked for dinner, but she presumed it was within walking distance.

◆ ◆ ◆

This had not been part of her plan. She had thought she would stay in Dartmouth, work in her parents' shop, perhaps improve her sewing and pursue that. She had not envisaged dates with Laurie every night he could get off, or meeting up in the moonlight by the bandstand, to sneak kisses when he wasn't meant to be away from his base.

She did not think about the future. They both knew that this relationship had an expiration date, even if they didn't say anything about it. Because all too soon he would be finishing his training, and leaving for some far off shore.

And Mandy would be forgotten.

She tried not to get too attached. But it was no use. The chemistry between them was electric, and the fact that they could not spend any real time together alone only made each kiss more desperate.

When Anya came home for the holidays, she dragged Mandy into her room when she had got back from a date with Laurie. The smile was still on her lips, and when Anya began interrogating her, her defences were down.

"You love him, don't you?" she said.

"I-" She hadn't said the words to him, and he had not said them to her, but she knew it was true. Heartbreakingly true.

"Yes," she whispered, the smile melting off her face.

"What are you going to do about it?" she asked. "He'll be leaving soon, won't he?"

◆ ◆ ◆

"I've got my date, for my first posting," Laurie said, and Mandy's breath caught in her throat.

She had known it was coming. They had spent the last three months falling in love, knowing that their relationship had an expiry date. They hadn't spoken about it. Mandy hadn't wanted to think about it.

"Okay," she said, taking a deep breath and avoiding his eyes. "When is it?"

"The second of May," Laurie said.

"That's soon," Mandy said, a sob catching in her throat.

"I know. Mandy..."

She took his hands in hers and forced herself to meet his dark, soulful eyes. "It's okay, Laurie. We both knew..."

"I love you, Mandy. I don't want to live without you."

Her heart jolted. She felt the same, but there was no answer, was there? He would be away on a ship, or stationed in some exotic place. She had never wanted to leave Dartmouth. Could she imagine her life there without him? No, not really. But there was nothing else she could do.

"Laurie..." she said. "We both knew..." But she couldn't get the words out. "I love you too," she whispered, because it was true, even if it didn't help anything.

"I want to show you the world. I want to experience everything with you."

Mandy swallowed, and then he slipped off the bench, and knelt before her on one knee.

And she gasped.

"I don't have it all figured out. I'm not sure how this will work or where we'll live or what we'll do. But I want to do it all with you. Amanda Moss, will you marry me?"

She hadn't expected the words. Sure, her sister and her friends had joked that they would marry, but she had rolled her eyes and not taken them seriously. He was leaving. She didn't want to. And surely that meant they were entirely incompatible, in the long run.

And yet...

She was in love with him. It had taken her far longer to admit it out loud than it had for her to feel it, but she had eventually told him, when he had told her.

But how could this work?

Her heart wanted to say yes. But her head...

"I don't see how it could work," she whispered, tears welling up in her eyes.

"Once I've finished my training, I could get a permanent post somewhere. We could start our lives together, somewhere exotic."

Mandy blinked back tears. "But you'll want to travel around. Be on a ship. You're going to be a naval officer."

"There'll be time at sea, yes. But it won't be forever." He took her hand and met her gaze, his dark eyes burning with emotion. "I want to be with you forever, Mandy. However we can manage it."

She swallowed. She didn't want to say no to him. But she couldn't say yes.

"I planned to stay here. To run the shop, to settle down, to have children-"

"I want to settle down with you. To have children with you. We can come back here, when we want a family. I can work at the college, I'm sure."

All these beautiful dreams were being laid out before her, and yet Mandy couldn't say yes.

"You'll resent me," she said. "When I want to come back here and you don't. You wanted to travel the world."

"And you wanted to stay here," he said. "So let's have both. Let's have everything, Mandy. I refuse to believe I cannot have everything I dream of. I have always wanted to be in the Navy. But my dreams have changed since I met you. And I cannot leave you behind to follow my old dream."

Laurie's voice was full of emotion, and Mandy did not think she had ever heard such romantic declarations before. The world seemed to stop around them as her mind whirred with the possibilities. If she said no... She would be saying goodbye to him, probably forever.

That was not something she thought she could do.

If she said yes... She would leave her beloved Dartmouth, yes, but she would return. She had never longed for adventures, but never had she expected to get whisked off her feet by a romantic sea-faring man who offered her the world.

"You think it can work?" she asked him, wanting to hear one last statement to wash away the doubts in her mind.

"I know we can make it work," Laurie said, and he rose up and kissed her so thoroughly that she was breathless when he pulled his lips away.

"Yes," Mandy said, before she had a chance to change her mind. "Yes, Laurie, I will marry you."

CHAPTER TWENTY-ONE

Mandy – 2020

Mandy closed her eyes and listened to Jonah playing the piano. He played one night a week in a local hotel, and she had started attending most weeks. She'd known him for years. He had taught her son Caspian to play piano, although Caspian had never been a natural, unfortunately.

Jonah played a mixture of classical music and classical covers of pop songs, and he always seemed popular with the patrons. Mandy had been to dinner with him more than once, but when he had suggested a relationship between them, she had pulled away. She had not been in a relationship since she had lost her beloved husband Laurie more than twenty-five years earlier. For a long time, she had not wanted to consider another man. She had her sewing, and her son, and she didn't need anything else. She couldn't have what she wanted – to have Laurie back – so she threw herself into every other aspect of her life.

The years had slipped by, and Caspian had become a man, moved away, moved back, and eventually married the wonderful Beth.

But she was too set in her ways by then to consider a second marriage. And the idea of feeling anything like she had felt for Laurie Blackwell scared her. It was far safer and easier to remain alone, living her life for her son and her extended family.

It didn't change the fact that she liked Jonah Owens. He made her laugh, and he flirted with her, and he reminded her what it was like to be young.

But then she would remember Laurie, and feel guilty, and decline another of Jonah's invitations to dinner.

The night was a pretty unremarkable one. The weather was drizzly and darkness had closed in early.

But for Mandy, it was night that would change the rest of her life.

There was a round of applause, and then Jonah began his next song. And Mandy's heart jolted in recognition. Her eyes snapped open and she watched him play Endless Love, emotion on his face. She wasn't sure where his emotion stemmed from, but she understood her own. It was her and Laurie's song. Always had been, since they had hummed it in that old bandstand and they had danced till dawn.

It felt like a sign. A sign that, after so many years mourning him, she should look to the future. A sign that he wanted her to be happy. A sign that he approved of her taking steps into the next chapter of her life.

So when Jonah asked her to stay for a drink after he had finished playing, as he always did, she did not say no.

CHAPTER TWENTY-TWO

Epilogue – 2023

Luca sipped at the glass of whisky his dad had brought up for him. It was only lunchtime, but he was not going to turn down the offer. In less than an hour, he would be marrying Isla, the woman he loved. He knew he wanted to spend the rest of his life with her, but it was hard to forget that this was not the first time he had walked down the aisle. He had thought then that he would be with Jessie forever. But fate had other plans.

He had been confident when he had proposed to Isla, and when she had then proposed to him, that he was ready to marry again. And yet now, with the wedding imminent, he felt a flutter of nerves in his belly at the thought of saying his vows again. What would Jessie think? Would she be happy for him? Or devastated that he had found another woman to love?

He had never expected to be a widow in his thirties. Who did? He wanted to make Isla happy. He envisaged their lives stretching out before them, hopefully full of joy and laughter and children. But he could not shake the memories of his past, the worries he would always carry with him.

Luca swilled the amber liquid in the glass and then took another sip. A knock at the door made him jump. He had told his parents he would meet them downstairs, in the hotel lobby. They would be marrying with a view out to the ocean, at one thirty that afternoon. He was glad his parents had managed to make the journey down to Devon. They lived so far away in the borders of Scotland, and their health was not what it once was. But Isla had wanted to marry in the place she loved, and Luca had been happy to oblige. He was rather pleased that he had married Jessie in her hometown of York. He wanted to try to keep the memories separate.

"Come in," he called. He was dressed, save for his cravat and jacket, so whoever it was wouldn't be shocked.

It was Luca, in fact, who was shocked at the face that peeked round the door. Wearing a violet dress and matching hat was Isla's aunt, Mandy.

He stood as she came in and closed the door behind her.

"How are you feeling?" she asked with a kind smile.

"Oh, the usual," he said, unsure why she was seeking him out. She was the closest Isla had to a parent at their wedding, but he hadn't expected to see her before the ceremony.

"I bet," she said, eyeing the glass of whisky. "I was sitting with Isla, when I thought that, as someone who has lost a spouse, you might be feeling a bit like I was on my wedding day to Jonah."

Luca was about to deny it. He didn't want his wife-to-be's aunt knowing the conflicting feelings that were plaguing him on his wedding day.

But she knew. She was a widow, and she had remarried. Perhaps she could help him to resolve the twisting and turning before he walked down the aisle.

"I love Isla," he said, wanting to make that clear from the offset.

"I know you do," Mandy said, taking a seat. Luca did the same. He wished he could offer her a drink, but he only had the glass of whisky his father had brought him.

"But it's hard, on a day like today. Not to remember..."

"It's very easy to get lost in memories," Mandy said. "And to feel unfaithful to them, too."

He nodded as she so perfectly described how he was feeling. "I'd like to think Jessie would be glad, wouldn't want me to be alone forever. But then I remember our vows, and what we promised, and wonder-"

Mandy reached out and put her small, pale hand upon his. "You don't want to lose those memories, Luca," she said. "But neither can you live your life through them. Believe me, I tried for many years."

He thought that over for a moment. "Can I ask what made you decide the time was right, to get remarried?" he asked. "Not that I'm going to change my mind," he said hurriedly. "I was just wondering."

"I wouldn't be up here if I thought you were going to change your mind," Mandy said. "I haven't told anyone else this, but I will tell you," she said. "The night Jonah proposed, mine and Laurie's song came on the radio. It's a song from the eighties, it's not played very often, and I had never mentioned it to anyone else. And yet it came on that night. It felt like a sign. Like Laurie was saying it was okay for me to move on. And Jonah had played it on the piano, the night that I decided to say yes to a date." She sighed. "You probably think I'm silly."

Luca shook his head. "No. I don't. I just wish I'd had a sign."

"I waited longer than I should have done," Mandy admitted. "Longer than Laurie would have wanted, I'm sure. You knew you wanted to propose to Isla. That is a sign in itself." Mandy glanced up at the clock. "I should be going. And you should be getting yourself ready."

Luca stood and put his hand on Mandy's shoulder for a moment. "Thank you, Mandy," he said. "No one else understands. I really appreciate you coming up."

"I'm very pleased to welcome you into the family, Luca. And I understand everything you're going through. But I am confident you and Isla are going to be very happy together. You can love someone with your whole heart, and then love again just as deeply. I promise you."

And then she was gone, and Luca's mind whirled with memories and wishes as he tied his cravat. He didn't have a best man, because there was no one he was close enough to ask. He had realised that he had lived a very secluded life since Jessie's death. Isla was a breath of fresh air. Everyone wanted to talk to her, and she was surrounded by close family who loved her. Her cousin's wife, her cousin's wife's sister, and a friend from when she had lived in London were her bridesmaids, with little Holly as her flower girl. Her cousin was giving her away. It was a thoroughly family affair.

He shrugged on his jacket and checked his appearance once more. His hair was neatly combed, his stubble closely shaved, and the light blue cravat was sitting straight. The clock ticked away in the background. Ten minutes until he needed to be downstairs. He wandered over to the window and looked out over the sea. Isla had wanted to marry with a view of the ocean, and Thurlestone Hotel had seemed like the perfect spot. The room they would spend their wedding night in also overlooked the sea, and they had planned with their photographer to sneak down to the beach and have some shots of just the two of them on the sand.

Although it was the height of summer, there had been drizzle that morning. You never could predict the English weather. But the sun had broken through the cloud, and he hoped they would still manage to have their outdoor photographs. His mum had told him it was good luck if it rained on your wedding day, and although he wasn't superstitious, he held on to that.

With a deep breath, he glanced at the clock one more time. Very shortly, he would be a married man once more. And he would start this next exciting phase of his life with Isla, in the cottage they had purchased together. It didn't have sea views – they couldn't afford such a luxury – but it was home. A home that they owned together.

And then he saw it. The brightest rainbow he had ever seen, arching across the sky, with one end on the cliff-top and the other jutting into the ocean.

His heart soared. This felt like a sign. A sign that Jessie was happy for him today. That this was all part of some great plan. He didn't know whether it was just because of his conversation with Mandy, but as he walked down the grand staircase to the foyer, his heart felt light and full of joy.

◆ ◆ ◆

There had been a time when Isla had never thought this day would come. Once upon a time she had dreamed of marrying Toby, but that had never happened. And now she was extremely grateful. He was not a man she should have tied herself to. It was just a shame it had taken her so long to see it. And that he had made her so fearful of other relationships.

But now... Now she had found the right man. Luca was the one she was supposed to marry, that she was sure of. Even if she had wobbled for a moment when he had proposed. Now everything was laid out in front of her. They had the house, ready to move into. They'd planned a short honeymoon to France, with her family offering to step in and help run the bookshop for the week they would be away. Everything was ready.

So why did she feel this annoying sense of panicky nausea? Was this what every bride felt like? She had never been one for performing, and there would be a lot of eyes on her today. Perhaps that was it.

Her bridesmaids – Beth, Lee, and Charlotte, her best friend from London – had helped her into her dress. It laced up the back, but it had proven harder to get on than she remembered. She hoped she would be able to sit down and eat in it without feeling terribly uncomfortable.

"You look beautiful," Beth said, as the hairdresser finished pinning in the veil. She had curled Isla's dark hair and pinned it up with a few loose tendrils to frame her face. The make-up artist had already worked her magic, and Isla felt like an airbrushed version of herself. Everything was perfect – well, except for this damn nausea.

"It's normal to feel nervous, right?" she asked Beth and Lee, her two married bridesmaids. Aunt Mandy had disappeared, and Beth hoped she would be back soon, before it was time to go down to the ballroom where the wedding would be held.

"Totally normal," Beth said.

"Even when you're sure, you're bound to feel nervous," Lee agreed.

"Okay," Isla said with a smile of relief. "I've felt so queasy, but I'm sure it's just nerves."

"I'm sure it's nerves," Charlotte said, fussing with the skirt of Isla's dress. "Either that, or you're pregnant."

She let out a laugh and then fell silent at the look on Isla's face.

Beth and Lee froze.

It was clearly meant to be a joke, but it sent Isla's mind reeling. She was on the pill, and her periods had always been erratic. But when had the last one been? Why couldn't she remember?

She felt the colour draining from her cheeks. Was it possible that Charlotte's joke was true? Could she be pregnant?

"Are you?" Lee whispered.

Isla swallowed. "I don't know."

"Don't think about it now," Beth said hurriedly. "This is your big day. You don't want to ruin-"

"It wouldn't ruin anything," Isla said. "I don't think... For me, anyway. It would be a good thing."

Beth smiled and squeezed her hand. "Good. But enjoy today first. Maybe don't drink, until you know..."

They all laughed.

"I'm lucky Holly didn't come out drunk," Lee said. "Didn't have a clue I was pregnant and I drank plenty of wine back then. I was terrified. I knew so much earlier with Harry, so it wasn't an issue."

Isla nodded, her head in a daze. Could she be carrying Luca's child right at this very moment?

Beth was right. It was better not to know now. Not

to wonder, not to worry, not to feel disappointment. She would feel joy today, and then they had the rest of their lives ahead of them to have a family.

Aunt Mandy reappeared, and Isla quickly dried her eyes. She hadn't even realised tears had built up there.

"Don't spoil your make-up!" Aunt Mandy admonished.

Isla laughed. There was an unspoken agreement that the possibility of a pregnancy would not leave the group of bridesmaids. Not until Isla was sure.

◆ ◆ ◆

"I now pronounce you husband and wife," the officiant said, a bright smile on her face. "You may kiss the bride."

There was applause from the crowd of family and friends who were there to see them get married, and Luca felt like his face might split from smiling so much. All of his earlier worries were gone. He loved Isla, and he was sure they were going to be very happy together. He would live in the present, because you couldn't live in the past nor know what the future held.

The kiss continued for longer than was probably appropriate, but Luca didn't care. When they pulled apart, she was blushing and smiling, and their friends and family were still clapping.

"Shall we, Mrs Martin?" Luca said, and Isla looped her arm through his.

They exited the ballroom, with their attendants following, and soon were busy with family photographs – which took a while, with Isla's extended family – and congratulations.

It was only when they went down to the beach for

their couple shots that they finally had a moment alone together, and Luca could ask Isla about the faraway look he kept noticing in her eyes.

"It's all a bit overwhelming, isn't it," he said, as they walked the beach hand-in-hand. The photographer was following at a distance, getting some candid shots.

Isla nodded. "It is," she said. "But I'm happy. Are you happy?"

"Ecstatically so," Luca reassured her.

"It's just-"

Luca's heart juddered. Was she having second thoughts? She had not responded to his first proposal, after all. But he thought they were past that.

"Isla?" He paused and turned to face her. He was dimly aware of the photographer in the background, but he needed to see his wife's face.

"Luca, I wasn't going to say anything. Not today, and not 'til I'm sure. But I can't stop myself."

Luca waited silently for her to say whatever it was that was on her mind.

"I think... There's a chance... I think I'm pregnant."

The world seemed to freeze for a moment. No woman had ever said those words to him before. He opened his mouth, closed it again, and then pulled her towards him and kissed her thoroughly, lifting her into the air as he did so.

"You're pleased?" she asked when they pulled away from each other. "If I am, I mean. I know we haven't planned it, but-"

"I am pleased," Luca said, his heart racing to catch up with the beats it seemed to have missed. "If you are."

"I am. If it's true, I mean. I don't know, for sure, but if it is..."

"Then I think it would make today even more perfect than it already is."

"Oh Luca," Isla said, wrapping her arms around his neck. "I love you. Do you think we could get a test today? I just want to know..."

"We can send someone out, surely? It's our wedding day?"

And then he whirled her around in his arms once more, and she giggled, and the photographer snapped several pictures that would grace their walls for the rest of their lives.

◆ ◆ ◆

"Everyone will wonder where we are," Isla said, as they slipped into their hotel room. Luca had got ready in it, and tonight they would spend their wedding night there, before flying to Paris the following day for their honeymoon. Isla had always wanted to visit the most romantic city in the world, and now she was getting her chance, with the man she loved.

"There are plenty of drinks and canapés going around," Luca said. "They won't miss us for a few minutes. And if they do, they'll just think we've snuck off to consummate the wedding."

Isla giggled. "Not sure that's what I want them all thinking about," she said. "You're going to have to help me, you know. This dress isn't very easy to manoeuvre in."

"You want me in the bathroom with you?" he asked.

Isla blushed. "No. But you can help me tie up the dress so it doesn't get in the way, can't you?"

By the time they'd managed to bustle up the voluptuous skirt of the dress – a feat that was planned for when it was time to dance – Isla's bladder wasn't going to hold on for much longer.

"Right," she said. "Give me that test. You read how we interpret it while I do it, okay?"

She shut the door behind her and awkwardly managed to do the test, before placing it carefully on the side and readjusting her dress. There were a few pieces of seaweed stuck in the netting of the skirt, but she didn't bother to remove them. There was surely sand and shells in it too, and there was no way she was going to get it all clean. After the wedding, she would send it to a dry cleaners, but for now she was just going to enjoy her day.

She avoided looking at the test. It needed to be left, anyway, and she wanted Luca to be there. Nerves bubbled in her stomach. She wanted it to be positive. That was a lot of pressure, especially on her wedding day. What if it wasn't? It wasn't as though they had been trying, she knew she shouldn't feel disappointed.

But she was also sure she would.

She opened the door and beckoned Luca in.

"Have you looked yet?" he asked.

She shook her head. "It needs a bit longer, anyway. Do you know what we're looking for?"

"Yeah, it's a cross on this one."

"Okay. Surely they should all be the same. No one wants to be confused at a time like this."

Luca laughed.

"If it's negative…" she began.

"Then we've not lost anything," he said, taking her hand. "This is just another unexpected twist, that we'll deal with either way."

Isla took a deep breath and nodded. "We should look now."

"Okay."

They both turned to face the counter next to the sink where she had laid down the all-important test.

The result was clear without closer inspection, but Isla still picked it up and held it up to the light.

"Is that-?" Luca asked.

Isla swallowed and nodded. "Looks like it."

A slow smile spread across Isla's lips, and she dropped the test onto the counter and threw herself into Luca's arms.

"I didn't think today could be any more perfect, but somehow it is."

◆ ◆ ◆

Luca had already felt nervous about the speech he would be giving. With no father of the bride in attendance, and no best man, his was to be the only speech. And although he was a confident man, he was not used to standing up in front of a crowd and speaking.

But Isla had wanted the traditional groom's speech and he had not wanted to let her down.

Now that he knew she was pregnant with their child, his mind was even more scrambled. He was thrilled, but he could not help thinking about how it was a milestone he had never reached with Jessie. A part of life he had never known with her. It was so strange that while experiencing something with Isla that he had already been through with Jessie, like a wedding, was tough, so was experiencing something entirely new.

Perhaps marrying again after a loss was never going to be simple.

He stood to a clinking of glasses and a hushing of voices, and took a deep breath. He had written his speech down, but his eyes wouldn't focus on it. He glanced out of the window, hoping to force his mind and his eyes to focus on the task at hand.

And then he saw the rainbow.

It was surely a new one. They had been outside since the rain that morning, and he had not seen it. But it was there now, filling the sky with colour and his heart with joy.

He looked down at his beautiful wife, and then around at their friends and family. His parents were at the top table with them, along with Isla's Aunt Mandy, Beth and Caspian. The room was filled with people they considered family, even if they were not all blood relations. Beth's sister Lee, her husband James and their children were sat on a table near to them, for they were an important part of their daily lives. Mandy's husband Jonah sat with them, and was being interrogated by little Holly.

This child they were going to bring into the world would be surrounded by more love and family that it would know what to do with.

"Thank you all so much for joining Isla and me today to celebrate our marriage," he began, knowing the silence had dragged on for a little too long as his mind wandered. "To Isla's bridesmaids, Beth, Lee and Charlotte, thank you for all your support in bringing this day together, and for standing by Isla's side. To my parents, and to Mandy and Jonah, thank you for supporting us both. And to Caspian, for stepping in to walk Isla down the aisle. I would like to raise a glass to you all."

Everyone joined him, and sipped their champagne in recognition of the family's hard work.

"And lastly, and most importantly, I wish to toast

my new wife. Isla, you have made me happier than I thought possible. I have known love, and I have known loss, and I did not think that I could be lucky enough to meet such an extraordinary woman and to marry again."

He glanced down at her, and then around the room, and he did not think there was a dry eye amongst them. He reached down and took Isla's hand and squeezed it tightly.

"No one knows where their life will take them or who they will meet. I just know that I thank my lucky stars every day that you walked into my bookshop dripping wet and asked for a job."

He raised his glass. "To Isla. And to love."

The room murmured the words back, and it was indeed a room filled with love. That evening, when they took to the dance floor for the first dance, Luca held Isla in his arms and wished he could bottle his happiness for a rainy day. They swayed together to the music, Isla's head on Luca's shoulder. He pressed a kiss to her hair and she looked up at him, love and emotion filling her eyes.

"Are you happy?" she asked.

"Happier than I ever thought I would be," he said, and lowered his lips to hers. Around them, other couples were invited to join in the dancing. Mandy and Jonah took to the floor, showing off some pretty impressive dance moves. Caspian and Beth gave a few twirls, while Lee and James swayed together in time with the rhythm. Luca's parents even made it onto the dance floor, and although neither was very nimble any more, they had forty years' worth of dancing together to fall back on.

◆ ◆ ◆

Wrapped in her new husband's arms and

surrounded by her loved ones, Isla had never been happier. She had thought her life was over when she had left London, but it had turned out it was only just beginning. Not far from the ballroom, the waves crashed on the shore as they had done in times of sorrow, times of heartache, and times of overwhelming joy. Things wouldn't always be easy, she knew that. But she was surrounded by love, and she would bring a child into a family that was so welcoming and accepting. And this baby would grow up in beautiful Devon, the place that had offered Isla – and Lee, and Beth – a home when their lives had not been going to plan.

And the waves would continue to carry the sand in and out, and the echoes of their love and happiness would reside in this place, no matter where their lives took them in the future. Because in this moment, in this room, in this county, this family was filled with more joy than they could have ever imagined.

◆ ◆ ◆

AFTERWORD

When I wrote the sixth book in the series, 'Summer of Sunshine', I thought it was the last book in the South West Series. But now here I am writing book 8! I do believe this is the last book, and that I am closing this chapter on this family – but never say never! However, I do have another Devon series in the works, because I cannot close the door on the beautiful county I grew up in. If you'd like to hear news of any new books, please sign up to my newsletter at tiny.cc/paulinyi.

Thank you so much for coming on this journey with me. These characters feel like I know them so well, and getting to go back and share some of Mandy's life, growing up in Dartmouth, has allowed me to learn more about Dartmouth from before I was born (thanks Mum for the help in researching!) Although we know that Mandy and Laurie do not get to grow old together, I was pleased to explore their romance, and then the idea of loving again, even after loss – a theme that is important for both Mandy and Luca.

I kept writing this series because of all your support and so thank you, again, from the bottom of my heart.

Happy reading, always,

Rebecca

BOOKS IN THIS SERIES

The South West Series

Fall in love in the South West of England.

The Worst Christmas Ever?

Can the magic of the Christmas season be rediscovered in a small Devon town?

When Shirley 'Lee' Jones returns home from an awful day at the office, the last thing she expects to find is her husband in bed with another woman. Six weeks until Christmas, and Lee finds the life she had so carefully planned has been utterly decimated.

Hurt, angry and confused, Lee makes a whirlwind decision to drive her problems away and ends up in Totnes, an eccentric town in the heart of Devon. As Christmas approaches, Lee tries to figure out what path her life will follow now, as she looks at it from the perspective of a soon-to-be 31-year-old divorcée.

Can she ever return to her normal life? Or is a new reality - and a new man - on the horizon?

Finding herself and flirting with the handsome local

police officer might just make this the best Christmas ever.

Fans of Jill Mansell and Sophie Kinsella are loving this romantic series.

Buy 'The Worst Christmas Ever?' and begin your journey to Devon today!

Lawyers And Lattes

A new home, a new man, and a new career are all great - but do they always lead to happily-ever-after?

Shirley 'Lee' Jones has made some spontaneous and sometimes questionable decisions since the breakup of her marriage, but deciding to remain in the quirky town of Totnes has got to be the biggest decision so far. Now Lee has a new business, gorgeous man, and friends keeping life interesting. But when questions of law crop up in her life again, she finds herself yearning for the career and the life plan she gave up when she left everything behind.

And when unexpected news tests her relationship, her resolve, and everything tying her to her life, Lee must decide between the person she is and the person she wants to become.

Sometimes decisions about life, law, and love all reside in grey areas. Will Lee's newfound happiness in Devon be short-lived? Or could her new life give her the chance to have everything she's ever wanted?

Feeling The Fireworks

Can Beth rekindle her passion for life and love in picturesque Dartmouth?

When Beth Davis made a whirlwind decision to move to picturesque Dartmouth to shake up her repetitive life, the last thing she expected to find was a passion in life - or a man who could make her feel fireworks.

A change in home and job seems like exactly what Beth needs to blow away the cobwebs that have been forming around her dead-end job. With little money to her name and no real plan, Beth needs to make things work, fast - without relying on her big sister Lee to bail her out.

When she meets the handsome, mysterious Caspian in a daring late-night swim, she instantly feels fireworks that she had long forgotten. Can Dartmouth - and Caspian - reawaken her passion for life and love?

'Feeling the Fireworks' is Book 3 in the South West Series but can be read as a standalone novel. Fall in love with Devon today!

The Best Christmas Ever

A Devon wedding with the magic of Christmas and a dose of small town charm - and the potential for a lot of family drama.

Lee Davis is about to marry the man of her dreams - and

at her favourite time of year. But she's finding it hard to feel the magic of Christmas or the excitement about her wedding as a face from her past reappears and worries about her second time down the aisle surface.

James Knight thought he had everything - the woman he was destined to be with, an adorable daughter and a happy life in the countryside. But with his wife-to-be seeming more and more distant, is he doomed to be jilted at the alter again?

Beth Davis is pretty sure she's lost her heart to handsome, brooding Caspian - but he's moved away to Edinburgh, and their fiery romance seems to have been stopped before it had truly started.

Caspian Blackwell wants to be excited about his promotion and moving to an vibrant new city - but his heart is very much back in Dartmouth.

Can a festive Devon wedding make this the Best Christmas Ever?

Trouble In Tartan

Beth Davis didn't plan on falling in love when she moved to Dartmouth - she just wanted to feel some fireworks. The problem is, she's pretty sure that is exactly what is happening - but the object of her affections is living 600 miles away in Edinburgh. As she tries to start a career as an author, downs a few too many glasses of wine and attempts to make ends meet, keeping a long-distance relationship alive proves more and more challenging.

Caspian Blackwell has never let his heart make big decisions - but he's sorely tempted when the distance between them begins to cause problems in his relationship with Beth. When he decides he wants all or nothing, can he really put this new relationship before his career? Or will he end up exactly where he always feared he would: heartbroken?

A tale of love, longing and a relationship stretched between coastal England and Scotland.

Summer Of Sunshine

A summer holiday can wash up a whole host of family dramas...

Lee Knight wants to relax on a summer holiday away with her husband, sister and brother-in-law. But her desire for another baby is not making it easy to unwind.

James Knight hates to see his wife upset, and hopes a trip away will make her troubles lessen. But with concerns about his father's health, he's finding it hard to be there for her as much as she really needs.

Beth Blackwell is sick to death of everyone asking her two questions: when is her next book coming out, and when is she going to have a baby. The first is proving more difficult than she expected, and the second - well, she's not sure whether that's the way she wants her life to go.

Caspian Blackwell is enjoying life as a newlywed in

Edinburgh - although in his heart, he's missing living in Devon. A spate of redundancies at work has him pondering his future - but he worries his new wife's heart is engaged elsewhere when she becomes increasingly distant.

Can sun, sea and sand send the two couples back into more harmonious waters?

Healing The Heartbreak

sla Moss thought she knew what love was.

But when her five year relationship ends in heartbreak, no home, and no job, she decides to take up her cousin's offer of a break in beautiful coastal Devon.

She expects sea, sand and perhaps some comfort for her shattered soul - but when she starts taking shifts at a local bookshop, could love be on the cards?

With the guidance of her cousin Caspian and the rest of his family, as well as the handsome Luca, can Isla heal her broken heart?

'Healing the Heartbreak' is Book Seven in 'The South West Series', but can be read as a standalone novel.

Dancing Till Dawn

As Mandy prepares for her life to change, her mind wanders back to her first love...

1983

Amanda Moss loves her small town life. She is more than content with her life in the coastal town of Dartmouth. While her sister yearns for big city life, Amanda is sure she will stay in Devon for her whole life.

And then an invite to the Naval College ball changes everything...

Will dancing till dawn lead Amanda to dream of a different life?

Jump between past and present and catch up with Lee, James, Beth, Caspian, Isla, and Luca as they prepare for Mandy's second chance in love and life.

BOOKS BY THIS AUTHOR

At The Stroke Of Thirty

Just about to turn thirty, Macy Maxwell is loving her life. A busy social life, interesting work and a decent salary, she thinks she's got it all figured out. And so what if she thought she'd be married with kids by the time she turned thirty? Life is easy and fun.

And then, the night before her thirtieth birthday, everything changes. A near-fatal stroke leaves Macy re-evaluating everything in her life, as she tries to heal and get back the woman she was before.

Will moving back to rural Northumberland, a stroke support group and a handsome shoulder to cry on help her to find the Macy she was - or help her become the Macy she wants to be?

Fans of Sophie Kinsella and JoJo Moyes will love this heart-warming tale of rebuilding a life, finding love and the twists and turns in life's journey.

'At the Stroke of Thirty' is book one in 'The Thirties Club' series, but can be read as a standalone novel.

Life Begins At Thirty

Amelia Rockwell has spent most of her adult life taking care of her terminally ill mother. She doesn't resent it - but it's certainly changed her plans for her life.

When her mother dies just after Amelia turns thirty, she's plunged into the depths of grief and confusion about what her life is going to look like. She struggles to keep up her friendships with the group of friends she sees every week in the local café, but finds solace in a grief support group, and in the arms of one particular member.

What started off as one night of comfort seems like it might turn into something more serious - but is Amelia ready to open her heart to anyone? And can she figure out where her life is going to go, without the support from her mother she'd always had?

Fans of JoJo Moyes and Sophie Kinsella will love this heart-warming and emotional tale of finding love and one's path in life.

'Life Begins at Thirty' is book two in The Thirties Club series but can be read as a standalone novel.

AT THE STROKE OF THIRTY

Read on for the Chapter One of 'At the Stroke of Thirty', book one in 'The Thirties Club' series. Purchase at: mybook.to/30sclub1

Chapter One

Macy Maxwell had never been in an ambulance before. But all that was to change on the day before her thirtieth birthday.

All in all, she had been rather well for her whole life. Even when she had been born, her mother had been home within a few hours. And no childhood illness or adult mishap had sent her for an overnight stay at the local hospital.

Not that there hadn't been one or two close calls. At eighteen, drunk on freedom and too much alcohol at university, she had fallen down a flight of stairs and fractured her ankle. But thanks – or not – to the copious amounts of alcohol she had been drinking, she didn't really notice how painful it was until the next day, when she promptly took herself off to A and E, and was home by the evening.

And now, at twenty-nine, nights out drinking were not so frequent – but not as infrequent as she might have expected. Was her life where she had thought it would be at the grand old age of twenty-nine? No, she supposed it was not. If she were honest with herself, she had pictured a good many things being in place in her life on the cusp of turning thirty. Husband; children; good job; owning her own house... So many things were not a reality.

But she wasn't sad about her life. She did have a good job – well, one she enjoyed and that brought in a decent wage, anyway. And she had fun going out with her friends: cocktail nights, fancy meals, shopping trips. And there had been boyfriends, on and off – but no one she could see herself spending the rest of her life with. She didn't own her own house, but she rented a snazzy flat in the centre of Newcastle, with a balcony that overlooked the river. Many things that felt like success – even if it wasn't the success she had perhaps envisioned.

It certainly wasn't the success her parents had envisioned for her. They still lived in the middle of nowhere in rural Northumberland, and whenever they rang, they asked whether she had found anybody, whether she was considering buying a house, and whether any of her friends had children. The not-so-subtle hints were hard to ignore, and hard not to take personally – but she had to remind herself that the things that she enjoyed in her life would not be things that they had desired for themselves. When an old friend from uni visited, she was in awe of Macy's flat, and the freedom that life in the city with a decent salary afforded her.

So perhaps her life was different than she expected – but different wasn't bad. Her life wasn't bad – in fact, many days, it felt like she had everything worked out.

◆ ◆ ◆

It wasn't unusual for Macy to spend an evening on the sofa with a bottle of wine and a takeaway, but that night she opted for pasta, tea, and a packet of chocolate biscuits.

She knew she would be drinking on the night of her birthday party – after all, one only turned thirty once – and so a quiet night that Friday night seemed like a good plan. Saturday, too, she thought she would spend quietly – perhaps organising the house, and making sure her outfit was ready for her birthday bash on the Sunday. She had even managed to book Monday off work, to ensure that she did not have to restrain herself in her celebrations, as well as having the Friday off as a birthday treat to herself.

Yes, everything was lined up perfectly, and although thirty had always seemed like a big milestone, she was finding herself more excited than scared about reaching it. It did seem rather grown-up; but then perhaps that's how everyone felt about turning a milestone birthday. Perhaps no-one ever really felt grown-up enough for the age they were. Except teenagers, she thought; they always thought they were more grown-up than they were.

She considered a film, but after flicking through the options available, she settled on binge-watching the latest medical drama that everyone was going on about. She was not particularly fond of needles or blood, but found she could watch these shows without cringing too much. She certainly could never have been a doctor or a nurse: far too squeamish. But it was amazing how several hours binge-watching a medical show could make you feel like you knew all the terminology, and by 11 o'clock, her head was full of terms she would probably never use again, and diagnoses of rare diseases that she ended up looking up on her phone to see whether they were even real.

Her phone buzzed twice during the evening, but other than that she had very little contact with the outside world. That seem to be the way of things, at the minute. Some days were full of social interaction: a day at work, surrounded by people, then an evening in the pub perhaps. Or a night out surrounded by strangers who became friends with the help of alcohol.

And then days like this where she saw no-one, spoke to no-one. She wasn't even sure she heard her own voice today. Perhaps she should get a cat, she thought – and then she remembered that her flat was not suitable for a cat, and she probably wasn't even allowed one anyway. And did talking to a pet really count as conversation? But maybe it would be better than not speaking for the best part of the weekend.

How was your weekend? Looking forward to seeing you on Sunday for your party! Mum X

Macy smiled. Mum still felt the need to sign off her texts, even after years of having a phone and knowing that her name came up when the message arrived. She was looking forward to seeing her parents, for it had been a while since she had last seen them. Somehow the distance between them, although not that great, seemed too much to travel for a weekend. Although it would mean a little more conversation...

She wondered how Mum and Dad would cope with her friends who were also invited to this party. She doubted they had met any of them before; people seem to come and go in her life fairly quickly, with no reason for them to be introduced to her parents. Old friends that remembered school trips and prom were in short supply these days.

But then Mum and Dad were usually fairly laid-back when it came to meeting new people. She doubted they would stay late – but she knew they'd booked a hotel room nearby. And perhaps they could go for a nice breakfast – or more probably, lunch – on the Monday, to make up for the fact that Macy was sure she would not spend an awful lot of time with them at the party.

Feeling excited and a little apprehensive about the big birthday bash, Macy decided to head to bed before midnight – which was fairly unusual for her – and get a decent night's sleep. Tomorrow would be the last day of her twenties and it felt somewhat momentous.

◆ ◆ ◆

Something was wrong. She knew that as soon she opened her eyes on the last day that she would be twenty-nine years old. The pain in her head throbbed like nothing she had known before and she was unsure whether she could make it to the kitchen to get a glass of water to take some paracetamol.

She had suffered with headaches before – fairly regularly, especially when she was stressed. But nothing like this. It was a struggle to even open her eyes, and so she left them closed and willed herself to go back to sleep. Had she been drinking the night before, she might've thought it was a hangover – but the most she had had was a cup of tea and a chocolate biscuit. Nothing that should be causing a headache like this. Perhaps she had not had enough sleep, she thought. Maybe if she could doze off once more, she would wake up and feel totally better. This was not how she wanted to spend today. A precious day off, and her birthday party the following day. She did not want to spend it in bed feeling miserable, especially with no good reason.

Half an hour later, when she opened her eyes once more, the pain had not dissipated. If anything it was worse, and she knew she could not avoid getting up and taking some painkillers. But as she sat up she realised with even more clarity that this was not a normal headache.

Her eyes felt like they were spinning inside her skull, and she was pretty sure she was swaying, for remaining upright seemed impossible. She tried to stand, took one step and stumbled, and then crawled towards the bathroom, wanting to cry, wanting to scream, but not knowing if anything would help. And then, suddenly, a rush of nausea – and she emptied her guts all over the hallway floor.

"Help," she croaked, but of course there was no one to hear her. That was the problem with living alone.

What was happening? She could not see straight, could not walk, could not stop being sick, and the pain in her head made her want to rip open her skull just to stop the throbbing.

She needed help.

But who could she ask? And what could they even do? What was this? A headache? Some sort of sickness bug? Some terrible disease? A brain tumour, perhaps? No. That was a dangerous path to go down. Diagnosing one's own symptoms always led to certain mortality.

So she did the only thing that seemed possible, and crawled back to her bed, yanking her phone from the bedside table where it was charging, and dialling 999.

"Ambulance, please," she got out, before vomiting all over the floor, and one of her legs.

◆ ◆ ◆

Never in her life had Macy felt so alone. A and E was busy, unsurprisingly, and no-one seemed to grasp quite how ill she felt - no matter how many times she vomited, or told them she thought she was going to die. The paramedics had started some sort of IV, and checked her blood pressure - and yet here she was, huddled in a wheelchair in the busy A and E, vomiting into a bowl and wondering how long she was going to be left there.

She wished someone was with her, if only to stop her panicking so much, or to go and ask how long she would wait to be seen - but there was no-one. Who could she call? None of her friends were close enough to her that she would ring them for something like this - and it would take her parents well over an hour to get here, and they would only panic. After all, it was probably just a dodgy prawn or something, messing with her system.

At least, that's what she tried to tell herself, as she sat there, watching the world going by and feeling like she didn't even have the energy to cry. The pain in her head was horrendous, the vomiting disgusting - but it wasn't just that. Her vision was a little more normal now, although not as sharp as she remembered. But her whole body just felt wrong. She felt as though she was not even well enough to sit there, in the wheelchair, to even exist... but there was no-one to even try to explain that confusing concept to, because she was left to wait.

She tried to take some comfort from that. The paramedics who had brought her in obviously didn't think it was that severe, whatever it was, because surely someone would have seen her by now if that was the case?

"Do you want some water, Miss?" a man's voice asked, and with difficulty, Macy lifted her head just high enough to see who was speaking. An older man, with short grey hair and a scruffy white beard was the one who had addressed her - and although water sounded like a good plan, she did not accept.

"No, thank you," she managed to say. She wondered if the police officers cuffed to either side of the man would have allowed him to get her a drink, if she had accepted. Why had he offered, she wondered? Because he cared about this woman all alone, terrified she was going to die in this waiting room? Or because he wanted a reason to move, to escape his jailers, to make them move...

At least he wasn't alone.

The minutes ticked by, but it felt like all concept of time had disappeared to Macy. It could have been minutes or hours later when a nurse called out her name; for a second, she almost forgot to respond.

"Here," she said finally, giving a weak wave. "Sorry, I can't walk..." She just knew that if she tried standing again, she would end up on the floor - and anyway, as the nurse came and took a rough hold of the wheelchair handles, Macy vomited into an already rather full sick bowl once more. She considered apologising, but didn't have the energy, and so kept her mouth shut.

Finally, she was wheeled into the inner sanctum, behind the curtain that earlier patients had been called behind. They reached a pale wooden door, and the wheelchair stopped.

"The wheelchair won't fit in the room," she nurse said. "You'll have to walk."

"I'll fall..." Macy said, taken aback by the brusque nature of the nurse while she sat so vulnerable, feeling so ill.

"You'll make it," the nurse said, taking the sick bowl from her lap and opening the door. Macy stood, shakily, and stumbled in, keeping low for fear of falling, and immediately collapsing into the chair next to the desk. It was no more comfortable than the wheelchair, and all she wanted to do was lie down, but there was another nurse here, and she only hoped this was a step in the right direction.

"Hello, Miss Maxwell. I'm Nurse Cranford, can you tell me why you're here today?"

"I think I'm dying," Macy said, tears rolling down her cheeks, as she reached out and gripped the desk. "Please, I feel so ill, I'm going to be sick-"

And then the first nurse returned, thrusting a clean sick bowl at her, and once more Macy emptied the contents of her stomach.

She tried the best she could to explain everything that had happened, all while wishing that the pain in her head could ease just a little. Surely soon someone would actually help her?

"We'll get you to a more comfortable chair," the nurse was saying, although the words seemed very far away. "And a doctor will come and see you."

"Please don't let me die," Macy whispered, and the nurse reached out and squeezed her hand.

"We won't. You're in the right place now, Macy, I promise. Now, Nurse Smith will wheel you to the assessment area."

And then, just like that, the wheelchair was in the room - and Macy almost fell into it, before throwing up yet again.

Could they not see how ill she was? Or was her mind simply playing tricks on her? Was this nothing, as they all seemed to be pretending it was?

She could only hope so.

◆ ◆ ◆

The next chair she fell into did at least recline. She felt like even sitting up was too much effort. The pain in her head had not subsided, and as they put in a cannula - which under normal circumstances would probably have caused her a decent amount of anxiety, but now was simply something she had to deal with - she hoped they could give her something for the pain soon.

And, she thought as she emptied her stomach yet again, something for the vomiting.

She lost count of how many doctors and nurses she spoke to. Finally some medication from a drip stopped her vomiting, but the paracetamol offered wasn't really cutting through the pain. Even existing seemed to hurt, and the black cloud of death did not disappear from her mind. Something terrible was wrong, she was sure - but no-one seemed to know what.

Eventually sleep seemed to come, and it was the only relief she'd had in hours - but then someone came to wake her up, and check her vitals, and the hell started all over again.

She realised she should probably tell someone where she was, but the thought of even looking at her phone made her want to be sick, in spite of the medication running through her veins to stop that.

"Miss Maxwell?" a young doctor asked, pulling aside the curtain. "How are you feeling? I'm Doctor Jennet."

"Not good," she said, trying to sit up but finding it a challenge.

"Is it the worst headache you have ever had? I see here

that you have suffered from migraines before."

"The worst ever," she said. "And I just feel so ill..."

He nodded. "Can you scrunch your eyes tight? Now open them. Now can you squeeze my hands, as tight as you can? Okay, pull me in, now push me away..."

It carried on for some minutes, with tasks that weren't difficult to accomplish but did not help Macy's terrible headache.

"Is there anything else I can take for the pain?" she asked, when he seemed to be done with her for now.

"I'll have a look into it," he promised.

She nodded dolefully, and then once again she was alone, trying to take comfort in the fact that no-one seemed too worried.

But then why did she feel so terrible?

◆ ◆ ◆

Eight hours had passed since she had entered A and E, by the time a decision was made, and she still had not felt well enough to look at her phone. The large analogue clock on the wall, however, told her that most of the day had gone, and yet she was still here, and still wondering what was making her feel so rotten.

"Miss Maxwell," the doctor said, almost announcing himself with her name as he drew the curtain open. "I have spoken with the other doctors, and believe you are suffering from a migraine. There is no suggestion that you need any scans - just plenty of rest at home."

"A migraine?"

He nodded.

"They can be this bad?" Relief washed over her, and then disbelief. She had suffered from migraines before, in her teenage years - and never had she felt anything like this.

"They can be, yes."

"How long will it last?"

"It can be up to three days," he said. "But hopefully not that long. Keep taking paracetamol, plenty of fluids, and rest."

"And if it doesn't go away?"

"I'm sure it will," he said, with far more confidence than Macy could muster to believe him. "But if it gets worse, or your experience any numbness or loss of function or vision, then come back here."

She nodded, struggling to take it all in. How was she going to go home, feeling like this? Although the thought of sleeping for twelve hours straight in her own bed was a lovely one. But the pain... in her head, her neck, her whole body. If she felt well enough, perhaps a bath would have been nice - but she wasn't sure how she would get up the stairs at home, let alone get in a bath.

"Is there anyone at home to keep any eye on you?"

She shook her head, and felt tears threatening to overwhelm her. It had been a very long day, and the following day was her thirtieth birthday - and here she was, alone and feeling more ill than she had ever felt in her life.

"Perhaps you might want to call a friend," he said. "Ask them to pop in and check on you..."

She nodded, before realising how painful that was, and stopped.

"I'll get your discharge paperwork sorted, and then you're free to go," he said.

How could leaving hospital be such an unappealing thought?

At least it was only a migraine, she thought; that was a comfort. It would pass; nothing had given them any cause for concern, and she had seen enough doctors and nurses for someone to pick up on any problem, surely?

A friend she could call to check up on her... that was a bit more challenging. She needed a lift home, really - the thought of a taxi was not appealing in that moment, and besides, they probably weren't that keen on picking up people from A and E. She was concerned the vomiting might start again, and then she'd have even more problems to deal with today.

There was Lucy, from work - perhaps she would be willing to help out. Or Alex - but she'd had a fling with him the previous summer, and so things were a bit more awkward now. Or maybe Toni, from next door; yes, she was the best choice, for at least she would only have to drive home. And maybe she had noticed the ambulance, and was concerned for her next-door-neighbour slash friend?

For the first time since ringing the ambulance, Macy pulled out her phone.

No messages.

No missed calls.

She sighed; at least no-one was sat at home, panicking about her, she thought.

Talking seemed like too much effort, but as she typed out a message, she realised the migraine was interfering with her ability to spell, and to think of the right words. Eventually though, she had a message that was understandable, and hit send, hoping Toni had her phone in sight.

Had terrible migraine. In hospital. Any chance you could pick me up? Would really appreciate it. Thanks. M x

A reply came seconds later, and Macy forced her eyes to focus on the words. At least her vision seemed better now.

OMG hun are you ok? Of course! Shall I leave now?

◆ ◆ ◆

Hunched over and struggling to believe she could still feel so ill and be sent home, Macy staggered to the front of the hospital, and leant against the wall as she waited for Toni to arrive. It was evening now, and the air was cool, but it was a welcome change from the stuffiness of the hospital. Beside her, a man in a hospital gown pushing around a drip stand was lighting a cigarette. He was accompanied by a nurse, and Macy wondered if he wasn't really well enough to be out here. The smell of the smoke did not help her headache, but she did not have the energy to move away from it.

A siren wailed nearby, and Macy focussed on keeping herself upright. At least she would be home soon, and could sleep off this migraine. Then perhaps she could find something to ease it. Surely the pain couldn't last much longer? She had never had a migraine before that had not responded to painkillers or sleep... hopefully this one would become more typical soon.

Toni's blue Citroen pulled up in the layby in front of her, and Macy made her way to the door, wincing at every movement.

"Hi," she said, her voice sounding a little distant. "Thanks for coming."

"No problem. I couldn't believe you were in the hospital! You know, I thought I heard an ambulance this morning, but I had a heavy night last night and slept it off. And with your birthday party tomorrow! What a nightmare. You must be better though, if they're sending you home, right?"

"I don't feel great," Macy managed to say, as the river of words began again. The noise was making her feel worse, and she felt like asking Toni to be quiet - but knew that it would be rude to do so. Instead she focussed on breathing in and out, and on not vomiting. It was only a ten minute drive, she could do this...

Or she hoped she could.

"Are you going to be all right on your own tonight?" Toni asked as they pulled up in the car park for their block of flats. "I can come over, if you like..." Her tone suggested she would rather not, and thankfully, despite how ill she was feeling, she did not fancy Toni's company either.

"I'll be okay," she said. "I'll ring you, if I get worse."

"If you're sure," Toni said. "I'm still hanging from last night..."

Macy didn't have the energy to respond as she got out of the car and slowly walked towards the front door. There was no lift, but thankfully she was only on the first floor - although the stairs took three times the amount of time to ascend as they would have normally done.

Her hand shook as she put the key in the lock, and tears threatened to overwhelm her. This was too much. She felt too ill. Even knowing what the problem was, she still felt scared about what was happening to her. Perhaps she had some frozen peas in, she thought, to put on her neck, on her head, to ease this pain a bit.

"I need to lie down," she said abruptly to Toni. "Thanks."

"No problem!" Toni said, all too chirpily. "Ring me if you need me!"

Macy shut the door and decide the bed was too far. Falling onto the sofa as soon as she reached it, she pulled the blanket that was always somewhere nearby over her and closed her eyes.

Please, please, make it stop, she thought to herself.

◆ ◆ ◆

When she next woke up, Macy forgot for a moment where she was and what had happened. But the pain was still there, and when she sat she felt dizzy, and all the memories of the day spent in hospital came flooding back.

Her mouth was dry and she thought a drink might help her head, so she staggered into the kitchen and let the tap run until the water was cool and clear. And that was when she saw it: the clock on the microwave, its bright green digital numbers informing her it was 03:24am.

Happy Birthday to me she thought, as she downed some water and winced at the pain moving her neck caused. Every step felt like a trial, but she managed to find a bag of frozen peas in the freezer, wrap a tea towel round them and hold them to the back of her head where the pain was worse, before finally making it to her bed. The duvet felt cool against her skin and her eyes closed as soon as her head touched the pillow.

She was thirty years old, with a party that evening, and at the minute the idea of dragging herself to the bathroom was too difficult.

What a bad start.

◆ ◆ ◆

Constant beeping from her phone, where she had abandoned it in the living room, eventually woke her again, but she was not surprised this time that the pain had not subsided. When she sat up, the world seemed to shimmer before her, and so for a few moments she sat and waited until it felt safe to stand. It wasn't as bad as when she had called the ambulance, at least; she had not been sick again, nor felt like her eyes were rolling around inside her head. She wasn't better... but she wasn't worse, either.

Her phone was almost dead, wedged between the sofa cushions from when she had collapsed there upon coming home the evening before, but it had enough battery for her to flick through all the messages that were causing the beeping.

Happy Birthday!

The big 3-0! Can't wait to party tonight. X

Happy birthday old lady! X

She held her head in her hands, and let the tears she had been holding in flow free. She was cold, but the heating was too far away right now. She felt weak, but food was too far away.

There was no way she was going to be well enough for this party tonight.

So she did the only thing she could think of, and picked up her phone, dialling the only person she wanted around her right now.

"Mum?" she said, as soon as the call connected. "Mum, I feel so ill."

◆ ◆ ◆

"Oh, sweetheart," Mum said, as soon as Macy managed to open the door. "You look terrible. Happy birthday, by the way."

"Thanks, Mum. I feel terrible..."

"Did you drink last night? It's not a hangover is it?" Dad

asked, looking the up and down.

Macy slumped in the chair, finding standing to be too difficult. If she were honest, sitting felt too much like hard work – but lying in bed wasn't making anything any better either.

She shook her head. "No, I didn't drink anything last night. Haven't in a few nights actually." Somewhere inside she felt a sense of indignation that anyone could think she would be this ill with a hangover, but she didn't have the energy to sustain the feeling.

"Just checking," Dad said, as Mum tutted.

"I'll go make a drink, and something to eat – and then you can tell us all about it, Macy. You need something to give you some energy, maybe some painkillers, too."

"Thanks, Mum," Macy said, letting her eyes drift closed. She was vaguely aware of her father sitting down next to her, but conversation felt like too much effort right now.

"Never seen you have a migraine this bad," Dad said.

"Never felt one this bad," Macy said, through gritted teeth. The pain was definitely still there, and the nausea – but then she didn't really remember when she had last eaten, so perhaps that was the issue. At least Mum and Dad were here now. She couldn't even bring herself to care about the party that she knew Mum had quickly cancelled as they drove down here. None of it seemed important compared with how ill she felt. She was sure, in a day or two, she would feel totally normal, and be gutted that her thirtieth birthday had been ruined by this inconvenient migraine.

But for now all she felt was pain and despair.

CONTACT ME

I love to hear from my readers. Email me at rebeccapaulinyi@gmail.com or find me on Facebook at facebook.com/rebeccapaulinyi.